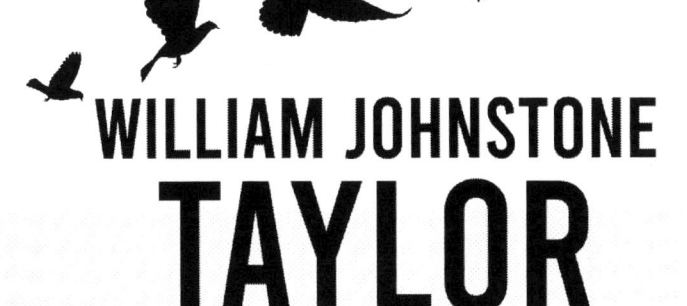

HOMEWARD ANGELS

A JAKE STORM ADVENTURE

WILLIAM JOHNSTONE TAYLOR

Homeward Angels Copyright © 2020 by William Johnstone Taylor

All rights reserved. No part of this publication may be reproduced, stored or transmitted in any form or by any means, electronic, mechanical, photocopying, recording, scanning, or otherwise without written permission from the publisher. It is illegal to copy this book, post it to a website, or distribute it by any other means without permission.

This novel is entirely a work of fiction. The names, characters and incidents portrayed in it are the work of the author's imagination. Any resemblance to actual persons, living or dead, events or localities is entirely coincidental.

William Johnstone Taylor asserts the moral right to be identified as the author of this work.

First edition

Cover art and book design by KH Koehler Design

ISBN: 9798666010167

DEDICATION

My great appreciation to the following folks without whose support these books would not be possible.
    K.H. Koehler, "Editor Extraordinaire"
    Helen McGonigle, Attorney
    Adria Henderson, Editor
    Gail H. Johnson, Research Assistant
    Foster Gamble, Editor
    Paul Nelson, Technical Assistant

CONTENTS

Chapter One..5
Chapter Two..8
Chapter Three..11
Chapter Four..17
Chapter Five...26
Chapter Six...31
Chapter Seven..37
Chapter Eight..42
Chapter Nine..48
Chapter Ten..57
Read an Excerpt of *Stolen Angels*..................................69
Read an Excerpt of *San Andros Fault*............................83
About the Author...109

CHAPTER 1

I was still dizzy from the meds the docs fed me earlier, but I knew we were pulling away from the hospital where I had been recuperating from a few wounds courtesy of some real bad guys across the border from El Paso. I had no idea what day it was or how long I had been under. Could have been a day or a week. I figured I would catch up by just listening to the folks around me so they wouldn't think I was still reeling and try to put me back into that awful hospital gown and restrict me to the all-white walls and antiseptic smell.

My friend Gage slid into the seat behind the driver of the big black Suburban SUV.

Gage was the reason I was still alive and successful. He is the world's most connected intelligence officer and has contacts in every organization on the globe. His office is in the Tech Laboratory located on Patrick Air Force Base near Cocoa Beach, Florida, right across the Banana River from my private island. He is one of my best friends, along with Ron Sorensen.

I sat next to him, and before Sorensen could slip in, First Lieutenant Sally Moore, United States Marine Corps, Reserves, was next to me in a flash. Sorensen smiled and sat in the front. I knew he was only teasing Sally as he always grabbed the front passenger seat so he could stretch out as far as a vehicle would allow his six-foot-six frame. Sally and her Captain, Val Cline—along with their Gulfstream V luxury jet—had been assigned to us for the last few weeks as we traveled around the world, looking for an abducted young lady we had just recently returned to her family. A long and successful and terrifying story.

Sorensen, also known as "the Tree," is my oldest living friend on Earth. We met in a beer hall in Vietnam and bonded right away. Sorensen and Gage have worked every major case of mine for nearly fifty years. I often wondered if they are my real live guardian angels sent down directly from the Golden Marine Base in the sky!

Before we drove off, he passed me back my backpack and the rest of my gear. I also had my pockets stuffed for the mission ahead. Grenades were bouncing around in the bottom of my pack, courtesy of Sorensen. His favorite surprise weapon!

Gage informed us that the Major had requested we meet him in Virginia for a short conference. I knew we had to get that out of the way. I also thought we needed to get moving on the information we already had regarding the location of more missing kids. I knew the Major would be full of advice and legal methods we should use in our endeavors.

The Major is an attorney and friend. I have worked investigations for him for the best part of forty years. I once compared him to the "Major" character in a movie we saw together and it stuck. His real name is Doug Partin, and he is the most important and successful Civil Rights attorney in the world. I have been his "get it done button" for a very long time.

It should be noted that I like to act first and ask for permission later. So far, the Major has let me get away with it. I get more done that way.

I asked Sally if she and her plane had been tasked to deliver us to the east coast. She told me that as far as she and Captain Cline knew, they were to stay with us until we no longer needed them.

I ran the various needs I had over in my mind and wondered if those orders would apply to a few days on my island with Sally, watching the sun come up over Patrick Air Force Base and setting over Merritt Island. We would have to fill the space in between those events with our imaginations. I turned a little to see her profile, from left leg up to the pretty face that smiled back at me. She stuck out her chest a bit more.

Oh, yes, Lord. Let me survive the next few days!

CHAPTER 2

During the ride, Gage told me that this matter was far-reaching and involved hundreds of important people across the entire globe. He said it would be months, if not years, before all of this was all sorted out.

I looked at him and thought of all the kids we had sent back to their families over the past few weeks. I didn't trust our Justice Department to protect those kids and their families and said as much to Gage.

He told me a special task force of uncorrupted recent graduates from the FBI Academy had been being assigned to the security. He himself had picked the seasoned leaders of those details. He was still working on it and should have it all worked out in the next day or so.

I squinted at him and he elbowed me a little too hard, which made me cringe. I trusted his abilities with my life. It was the rest of the world he was connected to that bothered me.

We drove into the Biggs Army Airfield outside of El Paso, Texas, and right up to our fancy ride. A Gulfstream V with all the bells and whistles and some secret modifications you don't talk about in public. Captain Cline, the senior pilot stood at attention when Gage opened the door and climbed out. She saluted him and he put her at ease. Sally, the junior officer and co-pilot, saluted Cline and greeted her with a "Good Morning."

Captain Cline stepped over to me and hugged me. I like hugs better than salutes. She told me she was glad I was there. I thanked her and she went off with Sally to finish the planes pre-op.

I noticed Gage was on his cell phone, as usual—and so was Sorensen. The driver of the SUV was standing beside the big car, looking at Gage. Gage gave him a one-finger-up sign and I knew Gage was destined for somewhere else. I needed a copy of his ledger before we left, and I knew he had one available. Washington was on my list of destinations, but I had a couple of stops I wanted to make before. One name stood out clearly in my mind.

Gage signed off on his cell. Sorensen was saying something about having a bad connection and cut his words off like a comedy routine. He then shut his phone down. I figured he was talking to his office or an angry lady friend. The latter was unlikely. Sorensen never left a lady angry or wanting!

Gage explained he had to head back to Florida and continue saving the world from derelicts like Sorensen and I. He said he wanted to be in on our debriefing to make sure there were no ambushes by any political plants.

I asked him for a copy of the ledger that Sorensen and I had taken from a very bad guy from Brazil. The guy, Frances Schultz was the kingpin and facilitator of many child abductions around the world. The ledger held the names of some of the biggest child-trafficking criminals in the world. He reached into the SUV and pulled out his canvas duffle bag. He asked me if I needed any cash, and I asked him for five bucks for gas. He thought I was serious and reached into his wallet. I told him I was only kidding and had a few bucks left over from the mission I had just been on.

He passed me a stack of stapled together sheets of paper. I scanned them and saw redactions. I passed the stack back to him and asked for a clean set. He took out another stack and said some of the names were so sensitive that it would affect National Security if they were leaked. I told him I didn't care much for the political spin and would deal with the country's security needs as soon as I had a spare lifetime.

I scanned the next stack and found it clean. I told him I would leave a bunch of names for him and his group to nail. I said, "After all, Sorensen and I are only two guys."

He looked at us, shook his head, and asked that I try to keep the collateral damage to a minimum.

I winked at him and said, "The Lord will work it out."

I could tell that that was what he was afraid of.

He told me there were a couple of new cell phones in my backpack and a clean 9mm pistol. He looked at Sorensen, and I figured there were a few more weapons in Sorensen's pack. Gage gave us both a hug, and then he was off in the big black Chevy and on his way back to Florida.

CHAPTER 3

The first thing Sorensen and I did was walk over to a convenient Dumpster and toss the new cell phones. I trusted Gage with my life, but we had no idea where the phones had been before he stuck them in our packs.

Sally and Valery were standing at the base of the stairway as we approached. Sally requested our destination, and I asked her to start by filing a plan to the Chesterfield County Airport near Richmond, Virginia. I figured I would start by making the Major happy. I wouldn't fool Gage for a moment. In fact, I was sure he had guessed my priority list long before I did. I sure wouldn't care to have Gage as an enemy. I'm afraid he would eat my shorts.

We boarded the plane. Sally was in the right front seat, banging away on her computer. She glanced at me and winked. It wasn't a "hello" wink; it was a, "I know our flight plan was going to change very soon" wink. She was right, but I wanted to look through the ledger for a while to see if I could figure out my Super List.

I knew that even if there was a large cover-up going on by some of the news bureaus, the major perpetrators would know about our efforts as soon as the Major broke the news. He planned to make everyone aware of a worldwide child kidnapping ring, and that his team had recovered some of the children. He would tell the press just enough to bait their appetites. I looked at these pages that had the power to change the world.

As we rolled out onto the main runway, I brought myself back to the mission at hand. I could see Captain Valery had the controls and was talking into her headset. A moment later, we roared down the runway then up toward the clouds and turned to the right to clear the takeoff pattern. A moment later, we climbed nearly straight up like a rocket and turned to the northeast.

I recalled our last flight on this plane and how close to disaster we'd come. I wondered how much security was assigned to the plane as it sat on the tarmac back at Biggs. Knowing Gage, it was significant.

I thumbed through the pages and saw the one name that had haunted me since first discovering the ledger. Admiral Peter Mason. Former Chief of Staff of the Armed Forces, former Director of the CIA, and, now, close friend and advisor to the Vice President of the United States. Admiral Mason was one of the most powerful men on earth. He sat on more committees than I could count. He was the Darling of every right-wing war-mongering group in the country. I wasn't sure a day went by without some news announcement about his day. It seemed to help folks sleep better at night knowing he was alive and well, and that he had shot two under par at some golf club restricted to only the rich and powerful. Everyone wanted to grow up and be him.

I also recalled he and his wife had adopted two infants from

Eastern Europe a few years ago. I remembered his wife going on TV and urging others to contact adoption agencies and save the orphans of the Third World. I wondered now if everyone else could order their kids from a list of children still home safe with their families. Angela, a child I rescued on a past mission, had been special ordered because her DNA matched that of a popular warlord's ill child.

I couldn't recall any public pictures of the Mason kids, but I was sure they were Super Achievers. I had visited with the Masons a few times and the kids called me Uncle Jake. I had not seen them in some time and wasn't completely sure the dated pictures were of the Mason kids—but I was betting they were.

The children's real names and origins were there in my hands. Both children were Lakota Sioux Native Americans and had been taken from a temporary foster home five years ago in South Dakota. They were brother and sister and were taken from their family for some meaningless reason because that was what the admiral had requested. He paid a million dollars each for the kids and a hundred thousand to some adoption lawyer in the Carolina's that appeared to specialize in these kinds of matters. I saw the lawyer's name on a couple of other pages I scanned. I also knew where the admiral and his family presently lived.

The admiral had been in Sorensen's chain of command, and I recalled Sorensen speaking with him regarding other matters we had shared over the years. The two pages in the ledger dealing with the admiral also listed his participation in several other abductions. It seemed he received a small fortune to facilitate smuggling operations in and out of the country that involved children and what appeared to be drug trafficking. All payments and descriptions of services were memorialized in the ledger.

I went forward and requested Sally alter our flight plan as soon as we were cleared. We would fly to the Capital City Airport just outside of Harrisburg, Pennsylvania. Harrisburg International was across the Susquehanna River from Capital City and had a lot of eyes I didn't want looking at us in case Mason knew about the ledger. Sally smiled at me as she wrote the note on her kneeboard.

It dawned on me that I knew very little about Sally. I had no idea where she was from or even how old she was. I asked her if I could buy her a cup of coffee and she requested permission from Captain Cline. Cline smiled her approval and went back to driving the plane.

Sorensen was sleeping, as usual, so I motioned Sally to the rear and into the galley. She poured herself a paper cup of coffee, offered me a cup, which I passed on, and sat down on one of the rear seats. It seemed she was prepared for my personal questions, and as soon as I asked about Lieutenant Sally Moore, she jumped right in with her life story.

She was born in Brooklyn, New York, thirty-nine years ago. (Wow. I was off by about ten years.) She was an only child and said her father was a lawyer for the City of New York. Her mother, who divorced Sally's father while she was very young, was remarried to a fairly well-off garment merchant. She had graduated from high school at sixteen and went right into college, married her first boyfriend in college, and had three children in three years. Two boys and a girl, all of whom were in college. She was divorced from her first husband and in the process of divorcing her second even as we spoke.

She spoke so honestly and thoroughly that I felt like I was interviewing her for a job. She went on to say she had been a commercial pilot for Gulfstream America out of Savannah, Georgia, for about ten years. She learned to fly at a young age and very quickly became qualified as a flight instructor for a flight school in Bridgeport, Connecticut. She related the various plane types she became qualified in and said she fell in love with the Gulfstream G-V. She was hired by Gulfstream to fly dignitaries around the world and deliver new aircraft to their owners.

I interrupted her and pointed to her Marine Corps emblem on her flight suit. I asked how she and the Marine Corps got together. She laughed and said she flew a few Marine Corps senior officers around the planet and, one day, one of them asked if she would consider joining the Marine Corps Reserves to put a bit more excitement in her life every summer. I laughed, too. She said she thought he was joking and then realized he wasn't. She spoke with her boss at Gulf and he gave her his blessings. That was four years ago, and it was the best decision she had made in a life of some poor choices.

The following summer, she went to an abbreviated Officer Candidate School in Pensacola, Florida, and then Navy/Marine Flight School in the same area. She snapped her fingers and said, "Instant Marine." She flew once a month out of Marine Corps Air Station Cherry Point, North Carolina, and MCAS Beaufort, South Carolina. The Marine Corps allowed her to count her civilian flight times against her mandatory Marine hours, and it works out well. Her three kids going off to college freed her up to handle special missions for the government.

I told her that Sorensen and I were certainly grateful for that. I thanked her for her service and told her she would probably earn her Captain's Railroad Tracks after this mission, but she said she doubted it. She said our mission was just a taxi service compared to some of the missions she and Valery flew. I was impressed with her, for sure. Now that I realized there wasn't as much of an age difference between us, I was even more intrigued. Certainly, my kind of woman.

I stood up and held my hand out for her. She pulled me to her and kissed me, a long, mesmerizing kiss right on my lips. I about blacked out for a moment. This certainly was my idea of a dream come true.

The most recent injury in my side was singing its swan song to me as I bent over, and the position was not doing any good for my other interested parts, either. I pulled her up and tried to get back into my mission mind as best I could. I was never afraid of dying, but, at that moment, I was asking the Lord to let me live long enough to experience this lovely creature one time—or perhaps twice—before He took me.

I led Sally back to the cockpit and went back to my seat. I did a quick check on Sorensen and saw his eyes were still closed, but his right thumb was pointed up for me to see. I agreed with him. Wow!

CHAPTER 4

A short while later, Sally came over the intercom and announced they had changed our destination and were about thirty minutes from Harrisburg. I figured I had better come up with at least a preliminary plan for our visit to Admiral Mason's riverfront home near Yocumtown, PA.

I had been there on numerous occasions over the years. I had investigated the Three Mile Island disaster for the Major many years ago and often wondered why the admiral would choose to live so close to the nuclear plants when he could live anywhere on Earth. At least he had the good sense to live upstream from the island, but he was right up the river and within full view of the island. If the reactors ever blew again, depending on the prevailing winds, his entire home and land could be completely contaminated and be useless for many years. Not to mention it would kill him and his whole family.

We landed on the north side and I saw the cooling towers jutting up from the small island in the middle of the river. It was just about the end of the fall foliage season, so the trees that could make the place look a little hospitable were all but bare. It resembled Chernobyl. I had missed seeing Mason's home when we approached as it would have been right under the plane as we landed on Runway Eight at the Capitol City Airport. I remembered the airport well from landing here numerous times in my little plane during the Three Mile investigation.

We landed smoothly and taxied to Volo Aviation. A smiling tarmac attendant directed us to a sweet parking spot right in front of the business office door and ran around, placing wheel chocks fore and aft of the wheels. Sally came aft and welcomed us to beautiful New Cumberland, Pennsylvania. She said the temperature outside was a balmy thirty-eight degrees with a ten-knot wind out of the north/northeast, making the chill factor thirty-two.

I looked down at my lightweight shirt, as did Sorensen, and figured we had better grab a rental and head for the nearest mall. Sally walked into the rear of the aircraft and came forward with two military field jackets, both sized extra-large. Sufficient for me, but it looked like a hand-me-down on Sorensen from his tiny sister. It covered him well enough, but the mall was still on the agenda. I reached down and grabbed a stack of hundreds so Sally could pay for our landing fees and space rent, but she held up her hand and said the government had a deal with Volo and the Airport Authority not to charge. She pointed to the Marine Corps Emblem on her flight suit, which was conveniently located right next to the now much-lowered zipper, showing a bit more cleavage that was totaling distracting. When she said, "government," I thought "breasts," but quickly jumped back to business and said that was great. She sure was a pleasant distraction.

The ladies busied themselves with post-ops on the plane while Sorensen and I walked into the FBO to rent a car and get a map to the nearest Burlington Coat Factory. While waiting for the car to be brought around, I walked out to the plane and asked Captain Cline where they would be staying. She pointed at the aircraft and said it had all the comforts of home and the FBO had a pilots' lounge complete with shower and head facilities. I figured food was available, too. She said that under the circumstances, she was not fond of the idea of leaving the plane unattended. I agreed and asked if we could get them anything from town. She smiled and said no. They would manage.

Her concern brought me back to the mission and thoughts of Mason's mansion. I wasn't even sure Mason's family was there in Yocumtown or if he even had the children any longer. I did recall a news story on the admiral and his family going on some vacation in the Caribbean that past summer. The kids were tagging behind their parents as they boarded a small yacht, so chances are they hadn't eaten the kids yet.

I looked out on the river next to the airfield and figured a boat landing was out of the question at the Mason Hacienda. I really had to put some thought into this, as I was sure the president had provided him with a security detail that would match the Secret Service in its ability. I wasn't sure I wanted to tangle with them—and I certainly didn't want to put any of them down. No, I needed to be careful about this little sortie.

Sorensen had reloaded his pistols, and I could see the bumps in his pockets that held grenades. I had left mine on the plane but had two pistols. The silenced .22 caliber and my trusty S&W Shield 9mm auto. I had put a couple of spare magazines in my pockets and a spare cell phone from a mission in Bangkok. I left the satellite phone on the aircraft and took my backpack.

I was all set—except for a plan. I continued to think about it as I walked back into the FOB service center. Sorensen held up a set of keys and motioned me to the front door. I glanced at the local map pinned on the wall and zoomed right in on Mason's twenty-five-acre plantation. As the crow flies, it was only about two miles or so from where we were. A plan started to form in my mind.

We jumped into the rental car, which had nicely tinted windows and all-wheel drive. The added traction might come in handy, should we need it. I rummaged through my backpack for my little red phone book. I had cleverly coded the many sources and contacts, and, in one day, Sorensen read it and broke every code I had perfected. I found the name I had been looking for, abbreviated to "Thunderhawk" for Diane Thunderhawk. I'm so clever.

Diane Thunderhawk is the name of a good—no, a great—friend of mine in South Dakota. She is probably the most influential Native American in the country. From behind the scenes, she does more to better the lives of Native Americans than any other leader I had ever had the pleasure to know. She sits in on every major Native American Committee from California to Washington, DC. Very respected and well liked among all who know her.

She answered on the first ring and I pictured her sitting in the small living room of her modest little home in southern South Dakota. She ran a vast empire from her cell phone. Diane has the ability to know what's coming in the next moment. Although I was calling her from a new, burner phone and number, she answered, "I'm still waiting for that new phone."

I make it a point to provide her with the latest technology in cell phones nearly every time I see her. She spends so much time on her phones that they look worn out in a month. I answered her by saying

I had one for her, but it had been so long since she granted me a visit, it was old tech now. She laughed and said the duct tape was wearing out on the one she had.

There was a moment of silence, which I had learned to grant her while she read my thoughts. She then asked if I was bringing home more of her babies. Over the years, I had found and returned hundreds of Lakota Sioux children that had been taken from their families and tribes in direct violation of the Indian Child Welfare Act (ICWA). It's a very long story that the Native Americans have suffered for many, many years. I had been helping to return these children for nearly ten years. I never stopped scanning the roadsides and yards across the country as I looked for those missing kids. When I see them, I recognize them right off! It's a very long story for another time.

I told Diane I had a lead on two and needed her help. I briefed her on the current mission. I could hear that she had walked out of her house by the gentle wind passing over the microphone of her phone. She never trusted the walls of her home with a conversation such as the one we were having. She stayed silent as I told her the names of the children, Star and River White Owl. Then she gasped.

I waited until she responded by saying those were her cousin's children. I gave her a moment more and told her their current names were Laurie and Samuel Mason. I didn't need to tell her anything else. As I said, she was able to see the short future. She asked where I was and I told her. She asked what I needed and when. Before I could answer, she stated that her cousin had the children's DNA information and fingerprints I had advised all of the Lakota families to record. I told her that was good and would be very helpful. She asked if I needed any photos of the kids and I told her I did. She had some on her phone and would send them right away. I thanked her and asked her to hold off calling or speaking with her cousin until we had confirmed their identities. I would call her within a day if I were able to see the kids and confirm that they were, in fact, Star and River.

I was pretty sure they were, as I had proof in my hands in the form of the ledger. I just wasn't sure they would be there in Yocumtown. I told her that I might need the White Owls to immediately get on a plane and fly to where I was. I told her I would provide the plane and could have them here in less than three hours. I again asked for her to hold off speaking with them until I called back. She said she understood and signed off.

A moment later, my phone vibrated and two pretty Lakota kids' faces appeared on my phone. I showed them to Sorensen, who was very familiar with the Mason family, and he nodded. They were clearly Laurie and Sam. I had been around them on numerous occasions over the last five years since Mason claimed he had adopted them. I should have known when I first saw them, but Mason and his wife had gone on and on about them coming from an orphanage in the Ukraine, and, so, I passed on any ill thoughts I may have had because I looked up to this great American patriot. Some patriot.

I asked Sorensen to drive to the mall so we could pick up some warm coats and perhaps a change of skivvies and socks. Sorensen had been on his phone while I was speaking to Diane and confirmed that Mason was at his home only a couple of miles from where we were. I was tempted to drive over there and smash the gate in. That was anger and embarrassment knocking on my brain for trusting and admiring Admiral Mason so much. I wondered if he had always been crooked or had gotten himself caught up in some shady deal and was then strung along by threats and manipulation. I was trying to make excuses for his actions, but every time I thought of a reason, I thought of how many resources were at his disposal to get out of those predicaments.

Sorensen and I were the perfect examples of his assets. We would have and could have made all his troubles vanish with a simple request. Then I thought of the kids he and his wife were raising. The couple knew about the grief the White Owls were going through and let it happen. No, Mason was bad. According to the ledger, he made a small fortune by facilitating illegal drug shipments and child abductions. He didn't appear reluctant to take cash in return. He needed to be brought down, and we were there to do it. First, though, we needed to get those kids away from him and home to their real families.

We wandered the mall for a while until we found a "tall man" shop for Sorensen. He bought a warm coat with many pockets, as was his style. Some skivvies and a couple of pairs of socks. I couldn't find anything suitable in that store so we hit Macy's for me. I found a coat and bought a couple of pairs of skivvies and socks. We needed to get a room somewhere to take a shower before changing. I checked my cell for motels. The Fairfield Inn caught my eye. It was just a mile from where we were. We drove there and rented two adjoining rooms for three nights. I hoped we wouldn't need that much time to accomplish our job there, but we could always leave early.

After we cleaned up, compliments of Mr. Fairfield's shampoo and soap, we found a small deli and had some lunch. I filled Sorensen in on my plan. I wanted to put eyes on the kids before I brought the White Owls in from South Dakota. The timing was going to be everything. I had no idea what Mason would do to the children if he thought we were onto him. At least we still had the element of surprise. We climbed into the rental and headed down to Yocumtown.

I remembered the route to Mason's home as we climbed up Interstate 83. Two exits later, we got off and drove down some side roads. I could see the cooling towers south of us on Three Mile Island and wondered again why Mason would choose to live there. Perhaps he liked the secure feeling that our government had beefed up the security on our nuke plants and other public facilities since 911. Being a close friend of the president would help stretch that security web a little north to include his home. I still wouldn't want to be living in those towers' shadows.

We cruised by the main entrance to the Mason estate at normal speed but saw no indication that Mason had changed any of his habits since the last time I was here. No gate guards or big black SUVs parked on the roadside. I saw no indication of a camera looking at the road or entrance. The second time we passed the estate, I asked Sorensen to keep driving up to I-83. When I spotted the commuter lot, I told him to pull in.

I had another idea running through my Brain Housing Group. If Mason was not on alert yet and had no idea, he might be the subject of an investigation, then a more direct approach may be better. I didn't want to charge into his house with guns blazing, nor did Sorensen. We didn't know how much Mason knew about Sorensen's involvement in the child abduction ring investigation. In fact, Sorensen's immediate supervisor thought he was still in Brazil, preparing for the upcoming Olympics Security. Mason knew about my relationship with the Major, but he may not have put two and two together.

I looked at Sorensen and asked him if he would like to bum dinner off the admiral. He smiled as he caught on and said that would be an excellent idea. The admiral had asked us to drop by anytime we were in the area. At the discretion of the president's friends, we had certainly done enough for him over the years. I reflected on the fact that some may have aided his skullduggery in the very matter we were involved in. I should have looked deeper, and now I felt foolish for being so naive when it came to the rich and famous. Perhaps I'd do much better when I grew up!

CHAPTER 5

I recalled that the admiral was an early eater. He would be sitting down for his supper between five and six o'clock. We had about an hour before we could conveniently "drop in" and crash his meal. We had a great excuse for not calling first. He changed his phones as often as we did, and the only landline he had belonged to the alarm system at his house. He certainly would understand us not sending him a message through his contact office in Washington. He knew we always maintained a low profile. It was what made us valuable to him.

I put a call into Gage and knew what his first question and message would be.

"Where are you? And the Major is annoyed."

He said the Major was calling him off the hook and had left numerous messages on my various phone contacts. I knew Gage was fully aware of where we were because he would have been following our aircraft's flight path and landing. He also had access to the same information we did in the ledger. Couple that with him knowing who lived in that part of Pennsylvania and the Admiral's memorialized involvement in our current matter, and that told me he was performing for an audience.

I told him we were visiting a sick friend in Alaska, and that he shouldn't expect us for dinner. He didn't miss a beat and suggested I check in with the Major and give Dave a quick call. He said all else was fine and to soon expect a very large shakeup involving many folks. A few of the minor players we had read so much about lately were jumping ship and were sleeping with their lawyers as they waited for the earth to collapse beneath them.

His coded message told me that a few of our ledger names were attempting to cut legal deals while the public knowledge of what we had uncovered was still at a minimum. What they probably were not aware of was that some of the government officials they were trying to cut a deal with might be perpetrators of the same enterprise.

I could care less. I knew the Major would find a way to get every name out there and would demand that every child still alive be brought home. His press conferences were sometimes like going to a religious crusade, including the big top tent. Everyone should experience a Doug Partin speech on Human Rights once in their life. You come away feeling like you've been completely vandalized of your place on Earth by the very people you've trusted and relied on to put things right. More pointedly—our politicians. I learned a long time ago to shut his words off after he got going or I would be just as furious as the rest of the crowd, screaming and demanding justice after every paragraph.

I signed off from Gage and called Dave. I could tell he was on the Island as soon as he answered. My house and island cell service were connected through a mini-cell that used the Internet instead of the local public cell towers. It made a clicking sound when it connected. (Then again, it could be NSA up at Fort Meade turning on their tape recorders, too.)

Dave, my friend and confidant, lived near my home on the Banana River and acted as my maintenance man and security when I was away on a mission.

Dave answered and asked the same questions and gave me the same message from the Major. I told him I was Tom from the pizza place and that his four black olive slices were ready for pick up. He never missed a beat and announced that there had been a couple of speedboats circling the island and a few binoculars on the shore looking over from the Merritt Island side. He said no one had attempted to land on the Island yet, and he felt that had something to do with his friends staring back at them.

I told him I was sure most of them were reporters we had dealt with and were probably looking for a scoop on the Major's press conference. I told him that the ones that weren't reporters may be extremely dangerous and not to stand too much in the open. I mentioned that a lot of folks were going to jail and were not looking forward to it. He understood. Gage and the Major had briefed him. I told him he didn't know the half of it yet.

The next call I made was to the Major. He didn't sound too happy when he answered but cheerfully asked if I had made a wrong turn on the way to our meeting. I told him I was aiming for Richmond and hit Little Rock. He managed a chuckle and asked how soon he could expect me. I told him I should wrap up my Little Rock business in a couple of days. He asked if I had any idea how hard it was to keep the news media satisfied with only a few teaser answers to their questions. I told him I wasn't in that department and, besides, I had heard his preliminary conference didn't get much print.

He laughed and told me not to worry about it. They would be crawling all over themselves once he started giving out copies of some of the documents, he'd come into possession of. I had nearly forgotten about the other documents we had found along with the ledger. It was so full of damning info that I was hardly able to think about much more.

He said he could handle the news guys but was concerned about some of the other, shady looking folks lurking around. He had ample security, but he was finding new names every minute in the documents and was starting to feel a bit paranoid. He said that many of the rich and powerful had to be feeling the storm coming and it wouldn't be long before they tried to bring down the house.

I told him I understood and would be there as soon as possible. I went on to say that I needed to cut a snake's head off before it was too late.

Next, I called Sally and asked her to standby to fly to Sioux Falls to pick up Thunderhawk and the White Owls. She told me that my wish was her command. I liked the sound of that and told her it may be in the next few minutes. I would call her and tell her I would meet her in Harrisburg as soon as she arrived. That would be the signal for them to get out to South Dakota and back as fast as they could. She agreed and signed off.

Next, I called Diane and asked her to drive up to Sioux Falls and stand by for my call. I told her if things went well—and I was ninety-nine percent sure they would—she was to contact the White Owls and have them grab all of their kids' documents and race to the airport. A big Gulf V jet with two female pilots would be waiting for them at Maverick Air Center. I wished her well and said I hoped I would get one of her great hugs in the next few hours. She asked if I wanted her to come, too, and I said certainly. I wouldn't want her to miss it for the world. She laughed, but I could tell she was anxious.

We signed off and I noticed Sorensen was driving and readjusting his weaponry at the same time. We had no problem bringing weapons into the admiral's house. In fact, I was sure he expected it. I was also thinking he might think we were there to protect him. I'm sure he felt so far above the law that no matter what he was involved in, the White House and the Intel community would look after him. It had also passed through my mind that the vice president himself might be listed in the ledger.

CHAPTER 6

It was just about dark when I signaled to Sorensen to head down the road. A few small snowflakes reflected in the headlights as we drove south toward the Mason estate. I told Sorensen that as soon as we were sure that Laurie and Sammy were Star and River, I would signal Diane Thunderhawk and Sally to get a move on. He and I would have to figure out in a hurry how to get a five- and a six-year-old boy and girl out of the house and to the airport unscathed. Not to mention ourselves.

Too soon, the paved road to Mason's estate came up on our left. Sorensen turned to me and said, "See you on the other side."

We knuckled and drove through the entranceway.

The driveway was about an eighth of a mile long and joined a large circular loop in front of the house. The lights were all on in the mansion, both upstairs and down. We stopped in front of the main doors and immediately climbed out of the car as we normally did.

The front door opened and a casually dressed man with a military demeanor came out of the front door and greeted us. I didn't recognize him among the regular security staff Sorensen and I knew. Sorensen stepped away from me a little, which told me he recognized the guy.

I said, "Good evening" to the man and continued up the steps. The man returned my greeting but kept his full attention on Sorensen. I asked if the admiral was in residence, and he replied that he was but was too busy for visitors at this time.

Sorensen looked at the guy and said, "Jake, meet Rick Vann, who is supposed to be in federal prison right now for, among other things, attempting to use his official capacity as a U.S. Secret Service Agent to reroute nearly one hundred million dollars from the efforts in Afghanistan to himself and, to my knowledge, unknown co-conspirators." Sorensen moved closer to Vann and added, "Rick, go tell the admiral we're here or I'll stick that pistol you're toying with behind your back somewhere you would find very uncomfortable."

Vann looked from Sorensen to me and then back at Sorensen, whom I believed was about to drive Vann into the porch deck. He then turned back to the front door. He started to close the door when Sorensen put his boot across the threshold and stopped it from closing. As he walked away, I looked but didn't see the pistol at his back that Sorensen mentioned, but I never doubted it was there if Sorensen said so.

About two minutes later, we heard footsteps on the tile floor getting louder as they approached. I recognized the admiral's gait. It sounded as if he were marching in a parade with the perfect click and clock of his heals. I was sure he was counting cadence as he stepped. *Left, right, left, right.*

The door opened and there before us was one of the most decorated and honored military men of our generation. He immediately stuck out his hand to me and then to Sorensen, inviting us in with a grand smile on his face. He led us to the right toward the kitchen and a small family dining room area that his family used for informal occasions.

I piped up and apologized for not calling first, but told him I wasn't sure we would have had the time to visit while we passed through. I told him the snow outside slowed us down a bit and, so, we decided to take advantage and say a quick hello.

He said that that was great and we were welcome anytime. I saw no sign of Vann or any other security as we approached the dining room.

Mason stood aside at the door to the room and announced us to his wife, Barbara. She stood up from the table covered in dinner dishes and serving bowls. There was no sign of the two children, nor were there any place settings for them. The admiral's plate was partially bare but Mrs. Mason's looked as if she hadn't touched it yet.

I walked to her and hugged her, asking how she and the kids were. She nearly choked out the answer that she was fine and the kids were doing well. I got a sinking feeling she was going to say they were away at boarding school or shipped off to a relative's house. Instead, she said they were in their rooms upstairs, having dinner with Martha, their nanny.

I smiled, inwardly relieved, and said that was great and I couldn't wait to see them. Barbara did a quick eye dart at the admiral and asked us if we had eaten any dinner yet and that there was plenty. I lied that we had and thanked her. I was starved, and I knew Sorensen was, too. The snack we'd had earlier at the hotel was only a temporary fix. But, we needed to keep this meet and greet as short as possible.

I insisted she sit back down and finish her food, then pointed to the admiral's place and asked him to do the same. He was trying to be jolly and a good host, but there was a lot of tension in the air. Barbara sat down.

Just to try to relieve the tension, I grabbed a dinner roll. I looked at Sorensen. He sat opposite me across the table but within a good view of the door back to the main house. A moment later, Vann came out of the kitchen with a pot of coffee on a platter with four cups. There were already cups on the table and, being a bit on edge and not to mention paranoid, I decided I would have a glass of water from the pitcher already on the table.

Sorensen took a roll and buttered it. It took one and a half bites and mine was gone. My other hand was already reaching for more. I ate my roll and took a drink of the water I had poured for myself.

Vann placed the tray he was carrying down on the table and walked back to the kitchen. He never made eye contact with anyone but the admiral. No doubt looking for some kind of signal.

I turned slightly in my chair so I could see the kitchen door as Sorensen watched the door to the main house. Things were certainly tense.

Mason asked what brought us to the area at this time of year, knowing both Sorensen and I lived in Florida. He said it was about to get real nasty outside and was thinking of heading down to his winter home in Fort Myers, Florida before it got too bad and he was socked in.

I smiled and said we were doing some sightseeing up in Harrisburg and were on our way down to York for a visit. He smiled and apologized for asking. I told him I was sure he knew our mission, as important and informed as he was. I thanked him for being so humble. He smiled as if I were right and told Barbara to get the kids so they could see their favorite uncles before we had to leave.

I looked at her worried face and told her I would like to come with her to surprise them. She did another eye dart at the admiral and smiled at me. She stood and let her napkin fall to the floor. She didn't bother to retrieve it and waved me to follow her. I resisted the urge to look at Sorensen in case it would give us away to Mason. I also noticed a brief change in the light under the kitchen door, which told me Vann was standing behind it, listening. I smiled and excused myself.

The house was massive in the style of a Southern mansion. A huge two-story center with three dormers on the front roof. A side wing on the left and right of the main house provided the family casual areas. We were on the right and the admiral's office and library were on the left. There was a massive grand staircase leading from the front of the house to the second floor. The rest of the first floor was dedicated to a massive "show and tell" Show. Huge living room. A grand dining room that was often converted into a ballroom for formal parties and dances. A large commercial kitchen and various side rooms used for meetings and minor gatherings. I was very familiar with the house and had stayed there numerous times. I had some pleasant memories of gatherings and meetings.

The most memorable times were the past few years since Mason and his wife had adopted the two kids. I'd thought the children so fortunate to be brought into all this wealth and comfort far away from the war-torn land of their births. I could feel the anger building inside me as I pictured the faces of the real parents' grief upon learning their children were gone and they would never see them again. I had to fight my emotions back as Barbara led me away from the staircase and to the small service elevator at the rear of the house.

She looked behind a couple of times and as we approached the ornately framed elevator door. She gave me the shush signal with her right index finger. I looked around and noticed numerous video cameras pointed in various directions, but not, to my surprise, at where we were standing. She remained silent as she pressed a hidden button in the doorframe that caused the door to slide into the wall. I looked inside the elevator and saw no cameras mounted there, either. She led the way in and the door slid shut without pressing a floor button. The elevator had three stops. The first floor, the second floor, and then the basement. But, without pressing a floor button, she remained quiet.

I looked down at her. She had tears running down her face. Finally, she took a deep breath and told me she needed my help. I tried to look concerned and took her small hand in mine. I asked her what was wrong. I again scanned the ceiling of the elevator to check for hidden cameras. She saw my eye search and told me there were no cameras or listening devices in the elevator. She said that Peter insisted on it being private so he could use it as a quick meeting place out of his security's earshot.

I told her she had better tell me her problem quickly because we would soon be missed. She started by telling me she knew how fond I was of her husband. She put her right hand over the hand I was still holding hers with and asked me to keep an open mind for a moment. She paused again, and I wanted to shake her and tell her to get on with it. Instead, I stood there, acting patient but about ready to push the second-floor button so I could remove all doubt of the children's identity. She then just blurted out that her husband was a very bad man and was, in fact, a monster.

CHAPTER 7

I didn't have to act shocked at all. I was expecting something far different to be her problem. Infidelity, sickness, or a confession that she was secretly in love with me. Something bothersome, but not what she was saying of her husband of over thirty years. We didn't have much time to play question and answer games, so I just asked her if it involved the kids. She stiffened, and, after another deep sigh, said, "Yes, and far more."

She told me they were not from the Ukraine, but from the U.S., and they had been taken from a foster care facility somewhere out west. We were using up too much time and I pushed the second-floor button after releasing her hands. She looked at the button and then at me, and I thought she was going to completely lose it. I told her not to worry but to act as naturally as she could. I then quickly asked her about the rest of the security detail for the house.

She said they had mostly all resigned the previous day for some reason that the admiral wouldn't tell her. Rick and two others stayed.

The other two were at the International Airport, readying their jet for a trip overseas. She didn't know where and Peter wouldn't tell her that, either. Yesterday, her husband had received a phone call from one of the vice president's aides. Whatever the aide told him put him in a near tailspin. It had something to do with a dear friend of his in South America who was missing. I knew who she was referring to and reflected on the fact I was responsible for his disappearance!

My suspicion of a high-level White House connection was digging deeper into my psyche, and I sure didn't like it being there. I quickly asked her who was on the second floor besides the kids and their nanny. She said they were the only ones right now. She said Rick and the rest of the agents lived in an apartment in the basement.

The door to the elevator opened and I did a quick look left and right. The long hall was clear. I held her arm a moment and told her to stay close to me as we turned to the right toward the kid's area of the "east wing,", as the admiral referred to it. It was actually the "southeast wing," as far as the compass went. I glanced down the stairs to the first-floor landing and saw no one. I could now hear the kids talking and some music playing softly from a television down the hall.

I asked Barbara about the nanny. She said her name was Martha and she'd been hired at the same time Rick Vann arrived, about six months ago. She thought Martha was Rick's girlfriend or relative, as she saw them together often, walking in the yard.

I knew who Martha was. Her name was Martha Grant. She was a former Washington, D.C. police officer gone bad. She was Vann's accomplice and had been sent to prison at the same time he was. The problem right then was that Martha knew who I was, too. Perhaps not an immediate problem, but one that I knew would grow when we tried to split with the kids. She was a very dangerous woman. She would not go down easily. I decided to play it by ear and acted surprised to see her. I adjusted my silenced pistol in my right hip pocket so I could pull it fast if needed.

I let Barbara precede me into the large playroom designed for the kids. The two jumped up from their little dinner table at the sight of me. I picked them both up and swung them around as they screamed out "Uncle Jake!" about four times each. They were beautiful children and looked even more like the pictures I had on my phone than I remembered. That was confirmation, as far as I was concerned.

I kept the kids behind my torso as I turned and said hello to Martha. I did it with a big smile. She gave me a half-smile, and I could see her hands were empty. I saw no bulges in her slacks' pockets, nor did she glance at any particular place, looking for a weapon. I could tell she wasn't surprised, so Vann had informed her that we were here. I wasn't sure how much she and Vann knew about the kids' origin, nor the admiral's other illegal ventures, but I was sure they knew something. Both had been sentenced to twenty years in federal prison about two years ago, and the only way they could have been released was by Presidential Pardon.

I asked Martha how she was and she said much better now. I wasn't sure what she meant by that statement, but I figured living in the basement of a mansion was better than a maximum-security facility out west. She asked me what brought me up to Harrisburg during this awful time of the year, and I replied that I grew up in Massachusetts and New Hampshire. Pennsylvania didn't compare once you spent a winter in the White Mountains.

The whole time she and I were speaking, I noticed she was turning slightly to her right and her right foot was moving back ever so slowly. I could see from the angle of her right hand that there was something in it. I was positive it wasn't a ham sandwich and remembered her proficiency with knives. She was known for her ability to accurately throw a blade and hit a target at thirty feet. Part of her conviction involved the stabbing of a police officer in Alexandria, Virginia, during some dirty deal.

I attempted to look casual as every muscle in my body tightened up. I was rudely reminded of the staples in my side from my recent injury as those muscles prepared themselves for some special maneuvers. I made sure Barbara and the kids were directly behind me, slowly lifted my left hand, and pointed toward the window to Martha's right.

Her attention was diverted just enough for me to grab my pistol with my right hand and, without removing it from my pocket, twist it up and fired twice. I tagged her in the top of her left leg and her right shoulder as she attempted to throw a small, solid steel blade in my direction. The blade fell to the floor right at my feet, and she sat down heavily on one of the kid's small chairs next to the table.

I pulled my silenced pistol out of my pocket and, trying not to alarm the kids any more than they were, held it low, pointed right at Martha's face. As calmly and pleasant as I could, I asked Barbara to take the kids into one of their rooms, never taking my eyes off Martha. I heard them shuffle off behind me and, only then, glanced in my peripheral vision, noting that Barbara was going with them and not sneaking up behind me with a baseball bat.

I picked up a cloth napkin from the table and threw it to Martha to press over her leg wound. All this time, she hadn't uttered a peep or a groan from the pain. I knew the shoulder had to smart, as I was sure the little magnum .22 had busted up the bone in there fairly well. Her right arm was useless and her left was acting like Hans Brinker and the dike.

I needed some time to get rid of Rick and to neutralize the

admiral. Just for good measure, I popped Martha once in each foot with my .22 to make sure she couldn't outrun us, and then considered putting one between her eyes. I decided that from the agony on her face, she'd been grounded. I stepped behind her and pulled her arms back. I heard the first groan of pain from her. I took another napkin, tied her elbows together tightly, and then used a third napkin to gag her. She whispered something threatening to me just before I pulled the gag tight. I considered the head shot option again. With any luck, she'd bleed out before she received any medical attention and solve any future problem for me.

I turned off the light in the playroom and walked to the bedroom that Barbara and the kids were in. I asked Barbara where the kids' coats were so they could go for a ride. She told me they were in a closet in the downstairs front foyer. I motioned for her to take the kids down the front stairs and wait for me or Sorensen to come and get them. She did not hesitate, took the kids by the hands, and went out into the hall. I walked in the opposite direction to a rear staircase I knew led to the back of the family kitchen.

As I walked down the stairs, staying to the edges of each step, I could hear the admiral speaking to Sorensen. He was upset about something, but I couldn't quite figure out what he was talking about. As I descended, I saw a movement in the shadows to the right of the door into the family dining room. It was Vann, and he was holding a pistol out in front of him and pointing it in Sorensen's direction.

CHAPTER 8

There was no doubt he was about to shoot Sorensen, so I put three rounds into his head as quickly as my finger could pull the trigger. He went down with a crash against some boxes next to the wall. Sorensen moved quickly out of his chair, and I saw his pistol come around the corner of the door a moment later. I raised my hands and he pulled his pistol barrel up. He looked at Vann lying on the floor and made some remark about him not being missed.

I stepped through the door into the kitchen and saw that the admiral was nowhere to be seen. I moved to the front foyer and saw Barbara and the two kids standing in the far corner, already wearing their coats. Barbara began to ask about her husband and I said he'd run off somewhere. Sorensen was already out the door, holding my coat up to me and pointing his pistol one way and then the other. I asked him to get the car running and open the doors.

I gathered Barbara and the kids next to the door and told the kids we were going to play a game of "Who can run and jump into the car the fastest." They were visibly shaken up, and I was not too convincing with my game proposal, but when I said, "Go!" they dove into the open backseat door. Barbara followed quickly, slipped a bit on the snowy steps, and slid in behind the kids.

I had no idea where the admiral was or what he was capable of as it pertained to his family. I was not taking any chances and turned off the up switches on the light panel next to the door. All the lights went off on the porch and the circular drive. I then ran and jumped into the front passenger side of the car as Sorensen took off toward the road. I asked Barbara to hold the kids down on the seat as Sorensen and I were doing in the front. We made it to the main road without vent holes appearing in the car and drove right back to Harrisburg.

I called Sally and told her we'd had a change of plan. Five of us would be flying to the previously discussed destination. I asked her to call Diane Thunderhawk and inform her that we were heading to her in Sioux Falls and had two surprise packages to deliver to their parents. Sally said she would get right on it and file a flight plan.

I asked her to file a phony flight plan, as I wasn't sure if the admiral was on the phone to every crooked asset he knew, looking for salvation. That included the Vice President of the United States and, with that, the entire U.S. Air Force and their very efficient fighter jets with pointy things sticking out from under their wings. Not knowing what the future could hold, I asked Sally where the closest Gulfstream sales office was located where she could borrow a different piece of equipment for us to travel in. She said that she and Captain Cline had already thought of that and that a friend of hers from Gulf was flying an older, used Gulf into Capitol City Airport from Teterboro Airport in New Jersey for us to use temporarily. She'd already heard it make one pass over the airport and could see it was on its final approach. Her friend would fly the V right back to New Jersey and hanger it there until we needed it again.

I thanked her for being on the ball and said we were ten or fifteen minutes out. She said she and the Captain were being secretive while they were at the Service Center so their actions would take longer to figure out later by any snoops. I could hear our new ride's jet engines screaming in the background through her phone. The last thing she said was that they would get the plane topped off and ready to go.

I continued to watch the cars around us as we drove, particularly the ones passing us. No one challenged us, but I had our guests continue to lay low on the seats anyway. The children appeared to be enjoying themselves like a movie adventure, including the anticipation of a scary part about to appear.

I called Sally back and asked if she could get the service gate open for us to pull right on through and up to the aircraft. She had the keypad code and gave it to me. I told her we were nearly there and asked if she saw any suspicious activity going on. She said it appeared clear and signed off.

As we approached the gate next to the FBO, I gave Sorensen the code numbers. The gate opened swiftly and we pulled through. Airport protocol required that you wait on the opposite side of the gate until it closed. It seemed to take twice as long to close as it did to open. I could see the new aircraft parked fairly close to our Five. It still had its navigation lights flashing and had a fuel truck snugged up to its starboard wing.

Sorensen held back a few moments while we did a surveillance of the buildings and taxiways near us. It was a fairly small airport and easy to scan from our position. We saw no other vehicles except for the ones outside the gate, and the snow hadn't accumulated enough to require any plowing yet.

As soon as the fuel truck pulled away, Sorensen drove up to the new aircraft's stairs. He jumped out and opened the rear driver's side door so our guests could climb out and skip up the stairs into the aircraft.

I had considered leaving Barbara Mason there and going on without her. I was thinking it might be a bit uncomfortable when the White Owls confronted her. Then I thought about her willingness to speak out about the admiral. I wanted to get as much information from her as I could—and possibly a sworn statement. The admiral was tight with hundreds of government officials, and Barbara's knowledge of these folks just might make our inquiry a little easier. I saw her sitting next to the kids toward the front of the cabin, and the kids looked as if they needed her comfort right then. That sealed it for me. She was going for a plane ride, too.

Sally briefed me on her conversation with Diane Thunderhawk. Diane would have the White Owls at the airfield as soon as we called and said we were on approach. Diane checked into the Country Inn and Suites near the airfield. I was familiar with the hotel and had stayed there many times. Her staying there gave me an idea.

There was no doubt that Admiral Mason would claim his wife and children were kidnapped, and then a countrywide hunt would ensue. It wouldn't take the government long to figure out where we were headed, even with a phony flight plan. I had spent a great deal of time in South Dakota, helping the Lakota Sioux Native Americans with their ongoing war with the state. That's another story for another time, but I met a lot of folks there, and I knew many of the folks around the states' airfields. I had flown my Cessna 182 out there and used it as nearly my only means of transportation.

There was an FOB office on the south end of the airfield called

Palomino Air. I had parked my plane there numerous times, and I knew the service center manager. His name was Chase, and he was a Vietnam veteran like Sorensen and I. I was not sure if Chase was his first or last name, but I had his cell phone number memorized in my Brain Housing Unit.

It was still fairly early out there when I called him. He answered on the first ring and, when I told him who I was, I had to listen to how much the Marine Corps was overrated and something about real men toughing it out in the Army. Same abuse I always received from him. He was a good guy and well decorated from his time in the service. Some years ago, I had him spend a week with me on my island. We sailed the Intracoastal Waterway and I showed him Cape Canaveral, Cape Kennedy, and all the bikini-clad beauties lining the beaches from Canaveral to Sebastian Inlet. I thought he was going to wear out my high-powered binoculars before he left. Good guy. Good, reliable friend.

I explained to Chase in some detail what we were up to. I told him we were flying into Foss Field and I would appreciate the use of his hangar and big Dodge Van. I had used his cars so much over the years that I felt guilty not making the loan payments on them. He said there was no problem and to call him as soon as we were in range. I knew he had a small apartment in his big hangar there and would only have to roll out of the sack to greet us.

While I was talking to Chase, Sally gave me the thumbs up. We were now rolling on the taxiway for the main runway. The snow had picked up, but it was still within the Gulf's acceptable limits, so we didn't need to be de-iced before takeoff. There was no other activity on the field and we took off as soon as we lined up on the runway. The Gulf IV resembled our V but was much fancier. It was a used aircraft, and it must have previously belonged to a rock star. It was decked out like a hippie caravan trailer, with bright colors and guitar designs on the walls. I was sure I would find that the toilet was made of gold as soon as I checked it out. It was big, but Captain Cline climbed through the snow-filled sky like we were in a rocket ship.

I used the head on the plane after we had leveled out and the seat belt signs went out. The toilet wasn't gold, but the facility was fancy. Even had a bidet mounted next to a full-size bathtub. I wondered how the weight and balance of a full tub affected the dynamics of the plane in flight. There was a full-length mirror next to the toilet, which was a bit out there for my taste, but I guess some folks might be interested in their profile while standing in front of the john.

What I did find interesting was the amount of blood I had on my shirt and trousers. I took off my coat and found I had been leaking a little from a previous wound. I needed to find a bottle of orange juice to refill my veins with energy. I put my coat back on and washed up some. The shower looked inviting but I had a few calls to make before we flew into Sioux Falls. I also needed to get as much information as I could from Barbara Mason before she disappeared from our company. There was no doubt that the admiral had many assets in South Dakota and, once he discovered she was there, he would be calling in the favors.

CHAPTER 9

I went back out to the cabin and walked to the flight deck. I asked Sally if any clean shirts were hanging around in the aircraft. I didn't care if they were hippie looking or not, but she said the drawers and closets were empty. I opened my coat and she grimaced at the sight of all the bloodstains. I told her it wasn't as bad as it looked and that I must have pulled a stable or two while playing badly with the other kids. She didn't even crack a smile.

I wondered if she now doubted my abilities as a great lover. Unfortunately, I was not all that great even before all the holes appeared in my body. There were no extra clothes, nor were there any overalls hanging in the pilots' area like there were on our aircraft—which was now on its way to New Jersey. I decided to wear my coat and endure the heat so it would not upset the kids.

I asked Sally where we were pretending to go as I felt the plane turn left to the south. I had not felt it turn west yet. She said they had put in a flight plan for the small field at the Marine Corps Training

Center at Quantico, Virginia. That might throw off some of the sky search and confuse anyone tracking us. We were about to enter Washington airspace and would turn to the west just before the restricted airspace over D.C.

We leveled out and, a moment later, I heard her request a change of heading. Sally tapped me on the arm and said that was her cue. She brought up the dash display on her side of the flight deck and began pounding in some numbers and letters a physics professor wouldn't understand. I left them to their tasks and walked back into the cabin.

I asked Barbara if she would come with me for a few minutes to the rear of the plane. I grabbed my backpack, gave Sorensen a signal to entertain the kids, and went to the large galley area. Barbara joined me after making sure the kids were settled in. She was beginning to look gaunt, and her hands were trembling. She held her throat and attempted to smile at me.

Barbara started by thanking me for saving the children. She hesitated and thanked me for letting her come along to reunite the children with their parents. I looked into her eyes and asked her to tell me everything she knew about where they came from and how she and Mason had gotten them.

She told me that she had always wanted children but that Peter was too wrapped up in his career for it. She was pregnant once and lost the baby. She began to cry and went on to say that she thought Peter had given her something that caused her to abort. Knowing what he did from his nefarious actions memorialized in the ledger, I would have bet on him killing his child rather than go through the inconvenience of childrearing.

She told me that after he retired and his friends in the White House were re-elected, he settled down and asked her if she still wanted to have children. She said she was far beyond childbearing age and knew he was talking about adopting. She also knew he meant getting a child through Francis Schultz, his friend from South America and a notorious child-trafficker. Her husband had helped the Brazilians win the Olympics bid some years before and, as a result, he was owed a big political favor. Among other things they received from Schultz, they were able to describe what they wanted in their "perfect child."

They sat down and looked through every magazine and picture book they could find. Peter even acted like he was enjoying the process as they searched for the best qualifications in their child. They finally decided on the Lakota Sioux children because they were beautiful and nearly disease-free because of the remoteness of their homelands on the plains of South Dakota. As Barbara told her story, she had no idea how dangerously close I was coming to my boiling point when I thought about the grief the families of these beautiful children felt. I just managed to keep my cool.

I pictured the nearly pure environment of the Pine Ridge Reservation and the little town of Hot Springs where Star and River were from. The small town was just to the west of the Reservation and snuggled in on the rise to the Black Hills mountain range. Barbara probably didn't know the children were not exactly from the plains area, but it was close enough.

She went on to say that once they had decided on the perfect child—age, sex, and the rest of their preferred attributes—her husband contacted Schultz and put in their order. She said she could lie and say she thought their child would be legitimately processed through legal methods from an adoption agency that Shultz was affiliated with, but she knew from the beginning that if it was through Schultz, the child would be procured through illegal means.

With Schultz's help, they made up a story that they were considering adopting a child from Eastern Europe and spread the story amongst their friends and associates in the D.C. area. Not long after placing their order with Schultz, he called and said he had located the perfect child and that he had a sibling that was also available.

She was ecstatic over the news, and the admiral also appeared excited. She went on to say they agreed on the brother and sister package and, shortly thereafter, Schultz arranged for them to meet him personally in Kiev, Ukraine. She knew the children were from South Dakota and that the Ukrainian trip was a ruse to cover up any suspicion of the truth. A small problem was Sammy's knowledge of English. He was very bright and spoke out frequently. He also asked for his mother nearly every day. Laurie was too young to remember her real family and she hadn't spoken any full words at her age. They had to keep a close eye on Sam because he could have spilled the beans about the whole affair.

Barbara went on to tell me, not only the truth about River and Star, but the other ways the admiral aided Schultz in his illegal dealings, from kidnapping to drug transport in the U.S. and Europe. I had turned on my phone video camera function and had everything she said on film. I also took accurate notes of all the names and organizations she spoke about. She was a human Wikipedia of the criminal world. Before I finished questioning her, I asked her if she knew about the dirty business of Schultz selling body parts. She looked genuinely shocked when I told her about Schultz's business of putting together the perfect DNA matches for those in need and with the cash to pay for it—and stripping the victims of their lives for the profits. I believed her when she said she was not aware of that, but she went on to say she figured many of the children and young people involved were made to perform sexual favors for the very rich.

She had been to a party in Rio where every old rich fellow had one or more young pretty girls or boys hanging on them. She could tell from the look on the kids' faces that they were not there willingly.

I had enough from her that I felt I could bury the admiral and thanked her for her honestly.

I sent her back to her seat and went forward to the flight deck. Sally said that we were just east of Fort Wayne, Indiana. We were going to stop there and switch aircraft again. She had learned from one of her friends in Savannah that someone had inquired about our Gulf V, now comfortably hangared in New Jersey. She said it wouldn't be long before someone figured out our switch and ran us down. She had arranged to leave our current plane at Fort Wayne and borrow a Cessna for the short trip to Sioux Falls. I told her it was good thinking and went back to tell Sorensen.

Sorensen said he had just finished an interesting conversation with River regarding his memories of his family. The boy remembered his parents and his young life before he and his sister were taken from their daycare school by two South Dakota welfare women. The child needed to be professionally interviewed by a child psychologist as soon as possible.

I told him I had a complete confession from Barbara and I didn't believe the authorities would need much more to place the admiral and his pals under the federal prison in Colorado for many years.

Barbara stepped to us and asked if she could tell the children about their destination and that they would soon be home on their reservation. I knew the kids didn't live on the "res," but thought it wouldn't harm them to have her tell them what was going on and answer their questions.

As we approached Fort Wayne, I put in a call on one of my many burners. Gage was born in Fort Wayne, so I thought it appropriate I fill him in on our progress. He filled me in on the latest rats that were jumping ship, trying to cut legal deals with the authorities, and the latest scoop on what the documents were revealing.

He told me the Major and his staff had put together packets containing documents and cross references from one perpetrator to another. It was amazing how many important people were involved, as well as how many were going down.

I asked him if he had any news regarding Admiral Mason. He said he heard the admiral had turned up at the vice president's home near Philadelphia but the VP had sent him on his way. A number of the vice president's staff members were implicated in the documents, but nothing so far that showed any involvement of the president or VP. Hundreds of documents still needed to be analyzed, though. I told Gage that we were only switching planes in Fort Wayne and needed no logistical support there. He said he had many assets there, just in case. I thanked him and told him I would keep in touch.

We touched down at the Allen County Airfield and taxied right onto the apron in front of Atlantic Aviation. It was dark enough on the pad that I could see the stars shining through the clear Indiana sky. The only lights on were a couple of security lights on the service building. Sally opened the hatch and lowered the stairs. She waved for us to come right away, and all of us, including the children, filed out and onto the tarmac. Only then did I see another jet parked in front of our plane with its stairs down and its interior lights on. There wasn't a soul around, not even any of the ramp guys that normally swarm your plane, looking for any glitches that would spoil your day.

Captain Cline, carrying her flight bag, walked over to the Cessna Citation. It was somewhat smaller than our Gulf IV, but a great looking aircraft, nonetheless. From the sticker on its side, I saw that it was a new 560XL Citation Excel. That meant absolutely nothing to me, but I was still impressed. I also noticed it had a red cross painted on its tail and figured it must be used for Air Ambulance purposes. Sally walked by, carrying her gear. She said she and Captain Cline, as a cover story, were assigned to deliver the plane to the Swedish Government. They would have no idea it had been slightly used for a good cause.

Sally buttoned up our Gulf and she and the rest of us boarded the Citation that Cline already had most of the way through its preflight. The inside was set up like a passenger jet, but I could see the quick-release levers that disconnected the seats to convert it to cargo or Air Ambulance purposes. I also saw that the hatch could be opened twice as wide for larger objects to fit through.

Shortly afterward, we were rolling back down the taxiways to the main runway and, without hesitation, roaring down the runway and headed west toward South Dakota. I looked at the children and could see the excitement on their faces. I knew they were not headed for the lavish lifestyle they had become accustomed to, but they would enjoy a lifetime of family comforts that money could not buy.

We were in the air ten minutes when I noticed Sorensen was already sound asleep, snoring away like a chainsaw. Young River looked over at me and laughed at the noises Sorensen was making. These kids were going to be all right.

It seemed like only a few minutes had gone by when Sally bent around and announced we were on approach to Joe Foss Field in Sioux Falls and we should belt up. We were all still in our seats and no one had moved since we left Indiana, so everything was good there.

It never ceases to amaze me how spread out the communities are in and around South Dakota. As I looked down at the ground passing under us, I saw only a few lights from time to time. Then, all of a sudden, we were above Sioux Falls and it was like a light show. Bright and blinking like Disney World. I had spent a lot of time in South Dakota and, despite its problems, it was a great state with many great people I was proud to call my friends. Then again, some folks here were not so much my friends. Some pretty nasty characters.

We must have been cleared to land right off, as Captain Cline did a direct, straight-in landing with no field circling. I called Diane on her cell and told her we had just touched down and would be heading right to Palomino Air. I asked her if the White Owls were with her and she said they were. I asked her to keep them with her at the motel and that we would bring the packages to her there. She agreed and signed off.

As we rolled into Palomino Air's service area, I spotted Chase out in front of our plane, directing us to a huge, open hangar. Captain Cline shut down one of the engines and continued to roll until she was completely inside and Chase had given her the crossed light signal to stop. She shut the other engine down and it was deathly silent in the interior of the plane.

Sally came aft and opened the hatch, lowered the stairs, and greeted Chase as he stood at the base of the staircase. I could hear him asking her if she was carrying a couple of grubby-looking former Marines. He offered to throw us off the aircraft if she needed him to. Same old Chase.

I walked to the stairs and asked what the foul odor was coming from his direction and he answered it was my breakfast he had scraped up off the road on the way in. We both laughed and he met me halfway up the steps as I walked down with a great bear hug. We passed some more sarcastic greetings when Sorensen appeared at the hatch, asking what the cat had dragged in. I told him that Chase had brought us breakfast. He laughed and waved inside for the kids and

Barbara to deplane.

After the not so pleasant pleasantries were out of the way, I asked Chase if the area was clear. He said that Airport Security had passed by a couple of times, which was unusual for this time of night. He must have had a remote control in his pocket, as the doors began to close as we stood there. Chase said his van was parked a couple of buildings over and that a friend of his was sitting in his car, watching for snoops.

I told him I would only need the van for a short while, but he had heard that song before. He was right. I did have a reputation for overstaying my welcome. I had once had to leave that very van in Denver and poor Chase had had to fly out to get it back. In this business, I never knew what the next moment will bring, such as when we opened the side hatch of the hangar.

Chase spotted them first. Two shadows reflecting on the ground from the back of the next building over. He pushed us back inside the hanger and pointed toward his office on the other side of the hangar.

The admiral had found us.

CHAPTER 10

I took the lead and signaled Sally and the Captain to drop what they were doing and follow us. They complied and all of us trotted to the far wall. Chase was speaking to someone named Denny in his walkie-talkie. He wasn't getting any response and, so, he put the radio back into his pocket. Sorensen had his pistol out and at the ready as Chase opened a small side door on the hangar wall.

It led to a small room. He then opened a door leading outside. Sorensen held him back and vanished into the dark. I stood in front of the group in case someone rushed the door. I had my silenced pistol out in front of me, ready for anything that didn't resemble Sorensen's bear-like look appearing at the door. A moment later, Sorensen's head appeared, and then his arm as he waved us out. I could smell cordite in the air and knew it was coming from the barrel of his pistol. We'd heard nothing because of his silencer, but from the look on his face, he had seen some action.

Our gang followed Chase into the next hangar over and then to the rear of that building. We stopped and Sorensen said there were a few greeters stationed around the grounds and they were not friendly looking. Chase tried calling his friend again and looked grim when there was still no reply. Chase pulled out his cell phone and called someone that he questioned about airport activity. He grunted, signed off, and turned to Sorensen and me and waved us a little distance away from the others.

He said he had just spoken to a friend of his over at the Passenger Terminal who worked in Airport Administration. His friend said some State Agents had taken over the airport security about an hour before, saying that there was the possibility of some terrorist activity at the airfield and for all local cops and airport security to stand down while they investigated.

I was familiar with the DCI—the South Dakota Division of Investigation—and, for the most part, had respect for them. Unfortunately, a few were not so nice. I had a feeling the "not so nice" ones were outside those hangars and they were up to no good. To order the locals to stand down was not a good sign. Certainly not a sign they wanted to negotiate. They didn't want any witnesses to their plans. I figured that was a direct result of the admiral's friends pulling some strings. That and the few names of South Dakota Rich and Famous I had seen in the ledger. Not a good combination.

Chase led us to a small room completely built of cement blocks. It was some kind of a tool room and had small windows looking out to the rear of the building. Once inside, I asked everyone to sit on the floor below the window level. I gave Chase my .9mm pistol and asked him to stay with the women and kids.

Sorensen slipped out the door and into the main hangar and vanished in the dark. I went to the same side of the wall and saw he had left through a side door. I stood there and listened. He returned shortly, holding a man by the neck like he was a rag doll. He threw the man down on the cement floor and announced he had found a rat hiding behind some cars and showed me a large, silenced pistol he had taken from the fellow.

I could tell Sorensen had hit him hard—most likely with his gun, as the man's eyes were a bit crossed and he was mumbling something about a train or truck. Perhaps I just didn't understand him at all. I knelt on the floor and searched his pockets. He had a pocket full of .9mm ammunition, a wallet with a private investigators badge pinned in it, and a South Dakota-issued PI license card. His name was Evan Brown. He was twenty-seven years old and lived in Aberdeen, South Dakota. He also had a small radio in his pocket with an earbud sticking out of it. It was on and the little LED lights were blinking. It must have fallen from his ear when Sorensen smacked him. I started to place the bud in my ear when I looked at Evan's ears closer and decided to pull the bud off and listen through the speaker.

As soon as I pulled the plug, I heard someone speaking and directing someone named Joe to check out a small building. Someone else jumped in and said the van was clear. A moment later, a voice showing some air of authority called Brown. He waited and then called again. I covered the microphone on the radio and pressed the transmit button a couple of times. The voice told Joe to check out hangar one and look for Brown. He went on to say Brown's radio was messing up so he must be in the hangar. The voice told Joe to shoot everything that wasn't him or Brown if they got in the way. Joe spoke a humorous 10-4 and signed off.

I wondered if these guys knew there were women and children with us. Sorensen ran quietly across the hangar to the opposite door from us. I could barely make out his shadow in the reflection of the exit lights. I saw him lean up against the wall next to the door as it slowing opened.

A quiet voice through the radio called for Brown again. Just then, I saw Sorensen reach over and grab a man through the door. He lifted him up and slammed him down on the cement. I didn't figure a normal human being could have survived that body slam and shuddered a bit, thinking how broken up the man must be. If he survived that, he would need years of therapy to move any body parts. I reminded myself to try to stay on Sorensen's friends list.

Just then, my own young ward, Mr. Brown, started to stir. I pulled him up into a sitting position and slapped him across the left cheek to get his attention. That did it. I put Mr. Brown's pistol silencer up against the end of his nose and told him that I would blow his head off the first time he lied to me. He nodded. I asked his name and he gave it correctly. I asked him where he lived and he gave it up right away. I then asked him his mission, and he said he was there with four other men to stop some terrorists that were flying into the airport on a private plane.

I re-adjusted the position of the pistol barrel on his nose and asked him what his orders were when he saw these terrorists. He said Agent Reader of Homeland Security, the man who recruited them, told them to shoot anyone they saw. I looked at him, as if I found it incredible, he would take an order like that. He quickly noticed my state of mind and said they were working for a division of Homeland Security. Mr. Reader told them that Homeland Security would hire them all if they performed well on this mission.

I told him to shut up for a minute. I wondered what was becoming of our country when grown, intelligent people were so full of hate as to find joy in killing their fellow human beings. I did my share of it but didn't find it enjoyable. The old saying that, "Marines didn't like killing. They just didn't mind it" was mostly a joke to cover up the memories that reflected on the inside of our eyelids when we closed them at night.

Brown said he thought he was going to throw up and did. There was no doubt he had a concussion and probably needed medical attention sooner rather than later.

There were now two shooters left, if I was to believe Brown. I dragged him a distance away from the pool of vomit he was lying in and told him to lay on his stomach. He turned over slowly and started to retch again. Once the spasm had stopped, I pulled his hands behind his back and tied them with a plastic trashcan liner that was on a cart next to the wall. I couldn't gag him, as he would drown if he regurgitated again. I sat him up, leaned him against the wall, and told him I would shoot him dead if he uttered a peep to signal anyone.

He said he wouldn't and I considered a smack with my pistol handle. I figured it would kill him if I did that and let him slide. I had him positioned so all he could see was the dark rear wall, so I quietly moved toward the front hangar doors. As I arrived at the doors, I saw some movement to my left. I could tell it was Sorensen by the size and the fact that there was no sound at all as he walked toward me.

I briefed him about Brown's story and he just grunted. We were both familiar with Reader. He was a DCI Agent that we often bumped into while we were seeking out missing Lakota Indian children. I looked forward to shooting him. Reader, for some unknown reason, hated Native Americans and was extremely brutal to them when he arrested them. He was suspected of killing more than a few just for sport. Many vanished and the trail ended at Reader's feet. He was a favorite of the State Attorney General and nothing ever became of any investigation of him by the state. He was somewhere just outside where we were, and I wanted him bad.

I wondered if there had been an order to kill us from back east or if that was Reader's idea. Whoever gave the order had us in the perfect spot to be observed. Sorensen and I being put down in South Dakota would break very few hearts. I pictured our bodies on display in the front window of Well's Drug Emporium, stuffed in caskets tilted up for better viewing.

I told Sorensen I would go back to the rear of the hangar and watch the two access ways there. He could monitor the two front hangar doors. As I moved away, I heard Reader's voice tell someone to meet him at the fence in the parking lot. I stayed next to Sorensen until they finished speaking. I knew the parking lot near the fence was right behind the building we were in. I pointed to the rear side doors and we ran toward them. Sorensen went right and I went left. I glanced at the door to the little room where Chase and company were and saw Sally looking out at me as I turned to the side door. I gave her the "get down" signal with my hand and slipped out the side door.

The only lights were coming from the parking lot, but I could see a pair of security lights sticking out from the rear corner of the building. I was sure they would come on as soon as they sensed my movement.

I stayed close to the building and knelt down when I saw a slight movement near the fence. I leaned out some and saw it was Reader. He was still alone, as far as I could see, and none of the security lights had been triggered. I hugged the wall and, as soon as I knew I could go no farther, I stopped and sent a mental note to Sorensen. I knew we had little to no time before reinforcements showed up to aid Reader—and then our gooses would be cooked.

I thought a strong signal to Sorensen and stood up, triggering the lights and getting Reader's full attention. He swung his gun around in my direction but snapped backward before he could get off a shot. I knew Sorensen had been waiting for my signal to make his shot, and he was totally in tune with me. I ducked back down, thinking there was still another hombre out there, but then relaxed when I saw Sorensen dragging a body along behind him.

I walked over to Reader and saw he was still alive, but just barely. He looked up at me and gave me the snake eye of hate. He had two holes in the front of his jacket, up high toward his throat. They were small .22 caliber holes and there was no telling how much damage they had done to his insides. Sorensen dumped his guy on top of Reader and, after relieving both men of their weapons, we ran back into the hangar.

I instructed Captain Cline and Sally to jump back in their aircraft, retrieve their borrowed plane, and skip back to New Jersey as if they had never been in South Dakota. Captain Cline said their superiors would cover them if someone confronted them.

I tapped Sally on the cheek and did my best Bogart impression of, "Here's looking at you, kid." She just smiled and they both ran out the side door to the next hangar. Chase ran after them and, a moment later, we heard the massive doors begin to open.

Barbara was holding the kids close to her sides, and all three looked wrung out. Sorensen reached down and picked up River. I lifted Star. We all walked back across to the big hangar, and I could see Chase hooking up a Tug 80 towing vehicle to tow the Citation out of the hangar. That gave me an idea as I saw another Tug parked outside the door. I told Barbara to take the kids and sit down near the wall. I then signaled Sorensen to come with me.

I started the little Tug, which resembled a steel box with wheels, and drove back over to the hangar we had left. I pulled around back and parked beside Reader and his pal. We grabbed them both and heaved them into the back of the tug. We did the same with the other three. I took a large piece of rope that was wrapped around the grille of the Tug and pulled it over them and tied it off to the rear hitch, holding them in a pile—Reader on the bottom, groaning.

I pulled the Tug around to the front of the hangar and pointed it toward the fence next to the airfield tower. It would pass by the main terminal on its journey to the fence in full view of the night workers and cleaning crew. Everyone sounded as if they were still alive, even the body-slam guy. They would get medical attention and the locals would question Brown. I was sure Reader would have a lot to explain about shutting down Airport Security once the investigation was over. Brown liked to talk and felt he was on a mission from the Lord. Then again, I wouldn't be surprised if he turned up dead in the morning from acute pillow inhalation.

As the Tug slowly began its journey across the airfield in slow granny speed, I heard the Citation crank up and roll away. We didn't hang around to throw kisses and wave, as we knew there would be trouble coming soon.

I called to Barbara and the kids, found Chase, and grabbed the keys to the van. He was closing everything down in his hangar and asked me to drop him off at a honky-tonk where his friends would swear he was all night.

We jumped into the fifteen-passenger van and, with me driving, made our way to the Country Inn and Suites off Russell Street. A quick drop-off of Chase and then we headed to the parking lot of the hotel. I had called Diane and asked her and the White Owls to meet us between the hotel and the restaurant.

As soon as we pulled up, the White Owls rushed the van and

pulled the door open. After the hugs and kisses slowed down a little, I asked them to get in the van, including Diane, and ride with us. I knew we were still in danger of someone confronting us and needed to make ourselves scarce. They jumped in and I had Barbara move to the front passenger seat away from the White Owls. I was concerned that once I introduced her, they might find it hard to resist punching her out. I couldn't just drop her off on a corner, as I wasn't sure she wasn't on a kill list like we were. Anyhow, she was a good physical witness to some of the skullduggery of our case. I drove up Interstate 29 and headed south.

The sun came up before we hit the Iowa state line, and I decided to cross into Nebraska and then back into Iowa. I drove the van to a hotel on the outskirts of Sioux City and parked in the parking lot. The White Owls ignored Barbara after I told them who she was. The kids sang her praises and said she was really nice. Star kept referring to her as Mommy. That didn't sit well with the White Owls, but they remained quiet and tolerant.

I called a taxi and ordered two cabs for our crowd. The cab company dispatcher said he had a large van in the area and sent it right over. We all rode to the Sioux City Airport and got out at the passenger terminal. I used one of my phony IDs and credit cards and rented a car for Diane and the White Owls. The White Owls had family in Nebraska, close to the Pine Ridge Reservation, and they would be there before noon. I gave Diane a stack of hundreds and told her to abandon the rental somewhere public and that I would take care of the expense from the rental agency.

Sorensen, Barbara, and I walked them to the rental car and bid them a safe journey. Mrs. White Owl watched the kids hug Barbara goodbye, and she put her hand on Barbara's arm and said something in Lakota. I wasn't sure what it meant, but it was said reverently, so I knew it wasn't a threat. I was surprised Diane didn't hold out for the new phone I owed her. I made a mental note to buy and send her one as soon as I could find an AT&T store. We hugged and I saw her spirit reflected in her eyes. A great person!

Sorensen and I went into the terminal and picked the first flight leaving, which was to Minneapolis-St Paul Airport. We purchased a ticket for Barbara. She would be flying nonstop to Boston, where she had a sister living in South Weymouth. I had the address and told her to be expecting a call from Doug Partin. I assured her that Doug's staff would protect her. It was her only chance to escape her husband's wrath!

Before we went down to the gate, we went outside and threw our hardware into a pond next to the building. I didn't see Sorensen throw the hand grenades I knew he still had in his pockets and wondered how that was going to go over at security.

We made our way to the gate. Sorensen had some kind of Federal badge and a fancy ID card that let us bypass all the security checkpoints. That was handy and kept our identities, even our phony ones, confidential.

After we landed at Minneapolis, I called the Major and told him we would be flying into Richmond to meet him. He asked me to fly into Baltimore instead as he was going to inform the media of a press conference there that afternoon. I told him I would be there, explained to him that Barbara Mason would be waiting for his call to testify as best she could, and then signed off. I told Sorensen about the plan, and he said he was going to fly down to his home in Miami and try to get there in time to watch the press show.

After we had purchased our tickets to our final destination and sent Barbara to her gate, we hugged and Sorensen said, "Don't get dead. " He then walked away, head and shoulders above the crowds around him.

I had managed a direct flight into Baltimore and, after a quick call to the Major, one of his associates picked me up in front of the terminal. The young woman passed me a large packet labeled "Press Release." Not "Blockbuster" or "Earth-shaking." I opened it about in the middle, read a couple of paragraphs, and was shocked at the details it covered of one of the government officials that I easily recognized. This was going to be quite a dog and pony show. I was beginning to wish I had caught a flight to Orlando, instead.

As we drove to some undisclosed area the Major and his folks had chosen for the conference, I called Gage to inquire of Sally and Captain Cline's whereabouts. He welcomed me back to society and told me the ladies were currently on the tarmac in New Jersey. They were about to fly back to their home base in Yuma, Arizona. A vision of Sally crossed my mind and then quickly faded as I continued to worry about our age difference. I thanked him for the info and told him to get some popcorn cooked to watch the conference. He said he certainly would and told me there had been a great deal of pressure on the networks not to air it, but that the president himself ordered it be shown on every channel controlled by the FCC.

That seemed to clear him a bit in my mind. I still wondered about the VP. Gage said there were so many resignations being submitted around the country that he wasn't sure the government could continue to function. I laughed and said it would probably run better unattended than it had. He said that Wall Street had asked the president to shut down the market for a few days in the interest of national security. I figured the market would do just fine on its own. After reading some of the big names in the ledger, I was sure there would be all new leaders within a few days anyhow.

Despite the uninteresting title of "Press Release," it was a blockbuster press conference. It was being held in a large sports complex on the outskirts of Baltimore, near Interstate 95. When we arrived, I saw the Major's motor home parked next to a wood platform. I could see several glass shields positioned in front of the podium, similar to what the president enjoyed at his public appearances. It may have belonged to him, for all I knew. I recognized about fifteen to twenty civilian-clad security men all around the staging area.

At the appointed time, someone tested the microphones attached to the podium, a big semi-truck pulled up behind the motor home, and the Major appeared, walking around to the podium and surrounded by his staff and a well-known female U.S. Senator, Jackie Lyons, a Democrat from California. As he mounted the stand, a group of his staff, all carrying what I knew to be copies of what I was holding in my hand—a press release outlining the conference and showing proof of the actions of the folks listed as perpetrators of various crimes—were passed around.

The media, many of them daily faces we saw and trusted for years, were thumbing through the release like maniacs. Then the Major began to speak. The entire crowd went silent. It was a magnificent outline of the crimes committed, and he presented it as only the Major could. With Senator Lyons at his side, there was no doubt history was being made at that very moment.

While the Major changed the world, hopefully for the better, I slipped out of the crowd and hailed a cab.

Jake Storm Will Return

READ AN EXCERPT OF *STOLEN ANGELS (JAKE STORM #1)*

CHAPTER ONE

"This is going to be a tough one, Jake. A hell of a challenge," my old friend, Doug "Major" Partin said in his gruff, all-business voice over the phone.

A hell of a challenge for a hell of a hellraiser, he was probably thinking. But, I had undoubtedly earned that name over the years.

I just knew, from Doug's tone of voice, that this was another big one. (A "black op" or something similar).

As usual, I replied to his challenge with: "What else is new?" He spoke very quietly into his phone and nearly whispered that a friend of his' young daughter was missing near where I lived in Florida.

All of my life, my fights were not for my own benefit, but to protect those who were young, passive, handicapped, or who could not otherwise defend themselves. In school, I protected kids who didn't have the talent I possessed with my fists. Hell, I'd had a permanent seat outside the principal's office at my grammar school. My adult years weren't much different from that.

I joined the Marine Corps at the age of seventeen because I was "guaranteed to be a fighter pilot." What I didn't know then was that the recruiter would've promised me the moon if I would just sign the papers. But, I didn't do that until the next morning, when I woke to find the Marine Recruiting Sergeant sitting at my family's dining room table, drinking his morning coffee with my mother. He already had her signature, and he was holding the pen out to me in his outstretched hand, which hovered just above the enlistment contract. The amazing part was that it was about seven o'clock in the morning and we were nearly sixty miles east of the Marine Corps Recruiting Office located in Orlando, Florida. He would have had to leave his home before five o'clock in the morning. That should have told me how hungry he was for recruits. (I should have asked for a Cadillac.)

Truthfully, I was not very happy about my home life at the time. When I was younger, my father had beaten the hell out of me with a belt almost every night up through my pre-teen years. My stepfather wasn't too fond of me, either. As a result, I had been working for a group of multi-agency Federal Agents in the Cocoa Beach area by going undercover and letting bartenders serve me alcohol as a minor in nightclubs. A close friend had brought me into the gig to get me out of the house at night. (That's a story for another time!)

Within a few days, I was on my way to Parris Island, South Carolina, and the Marine Corps Recruit Training Depot. There I was introduced to the three guerrillas who would teach me how to survive the rest of my life.

I did well in boot camp, and, upon graduation, I was promoted to Private First Class. Eventually, I was sent off to Camp Lejeune, North Carolina, for infantry training and then ordered to Pensacola, Florida, and flight school—which I never made.

On the day of my graduation from ITR (Infantry Training Regiment), a big, black staff car pulled up in front of the headquarters building at Camp Geiger. A very large man in a black civilian suit, white shirt, and black tie waved me over, and, after I did a couple of double takes over my shoulder to make sure he was motioning to me, I walked over to the passenger side window.

This very large gentleman introduced himself as Master Sgt. John Kemper, USMC, the Chief Investigator of Marine Corps Base, Camp

Lejeune, Criminal Investigation Department. Chief Investigator Kemper invited me to climb into the front seat of his car for a little meeting. He told me he had been waiting for me for a couple of months and was getting impatient.

Sitting there nervously in the front seat of that large staff car, I learned I had come highly recommended by certain government agents (never to be named) for a position with the United States Marine Corps Criminal Investigation Department. I told Kemper that there must be some mistake. I was on my way to flight school in Florida and, in fact, was currently waiting for my bus.

As it turned out, over the next few years, I came to perform, among other responsibilities, the duties of a Criminal Investigator and Intelligence Operative for the Marine Corps. I was given the opportunity to play in Southeast Asia a few times, which I gracefully accepted. There, I was utilized in numerous undercover positions, but you won't read about those war moves until later, and not the complete stories, as I'm sure some of my former Marine colleagues are still out there and still feeling victimized by my shenanigans.

It was 0630—(6:30 AM for you Army guys)—on a Monday the day the Major called about the missing girl. A bright, fall morning outside my beautiful island home on Isle Del Sol off Merritt Island, Florida. The Banana River surrounding my island, which I could see through the window, was as smooth as glass with an occasional mullet jump causing a few circles over the surface. My boats were perfectly still against the long dock, and I could see the water move near the transom of my thirty-eight-foot Morgan sloop, The Deep Secret. A closer look told me it was a small Manatee grazing on the bottom grasses under the boat.

I have a panoramic view of the east from my home office. I looked out over the Banana River and across to the western shore of

Patrick Air Force Base on the long Canaveral barrier island that stretches from Ponce Inlet to the north to the Sebastian Inlet to the south. The island is broken up by man-made canals and lochs at Port Canaveral, about ten miles north of my island. Numerous barrier islands from Key West to the north of Maine protect the mainland from storm surges and tidal shifts. I call my barrier island "Canaveral," as I am not sure it has a proper name.

I had just gone out to my west dock, which serves as a maintenance area for my two-small speedboats and the pontoon boat I use to transport machinery and other large items. As usual, I could see Dave Bright, my Island Keeper and good friend, skimming down through Newfound Harbor in his Boston Whaler boat. Dave has been my friend for about twenty years and helped me build my island home from a tent and into the four thousand-square-foot paradise it is now. He would rival Angus MacGyver for ingenuity. He can do anything!

Dave lives in a small cabin on the shore of Newfound Harbor right next to the Merritt Island Airport. He can sit on his front porch dock and look southeast to see my island and northwest to see my small hangar where I keep my single-engine Cessna 182. Dave is one of my most trusted friends.

Earlier, he slid the nose of his boat onto the beach in the same spot he always uses and tossed me my morning newspaper and a hardy, "Good morning, sir."

I caught the paper before it sailed by me and into the water and gave him a snappy Marine Corps salute. He had some groceries and a couple of packages in the back of his boat, so I threw the paper up onto the back lawn, grabbed a couple of bags from him, and carried them to the end of the dock.

As I was walking back to retrieve more bags, I heard my office phone ring. I decided to let the answering service catch it and continued back to Dave's boat. Just as I was bending over for more bags, the phone rang again. Apparently, someone was anxious to speak to me at this early hour, so I ran back up to the phone box on the back patio.

The caller ID indicated that it was my old friend Doug Partin. (His nickname is "The Major" from an old movie we had seen many years before.) The Major is a well-known Civil Rights and Criminal Defense Attorney who lives in California. That meant it was about 0400 where he was. It was totally unlike him to call me at this hour from his home phone. That spelled "Important."

I grabbed the phone before it went over to the answering machine again and immediately asked him if he had wet the bed.

He chuckled a bit but told me to start taking notes. I had to put him on hold for a few moments until I could run into the house and to my office. I signaled to Dave with a twirling of my index finger to stand by for instructions. He nodded and started hauling his goods up toward the house. Dave knew enough of my business to understand my body language. He knew that when the phone rings before ten in the morning, I'm probably on my way off somewhere. All he was waiting for was the signal: Plane or boat. He could have either of them ready in one hour, fueled up, packed with provisions, and loaded with my ever-ready packed suitcase.

I grabbed the office phone and my notepad and slammed myself down on my couch in front of my desk.

As soon as I picked up, the Major said, "Signal Dave the plane."

(Did he know my routine or what?)

Dave was looking in from the kitchen as I pointed my finger up. He nodded his understanding and walked back toward my bedroom for my travel bag. As he walked down the hall, I could hear him speaking to his friend at the airport FBO (the "Fixed-Base Operator"—an organization granted the right by an airport to operate at it), to get my plane out of the hangar and preflight ready.

The Major asked me if I was ready to take notes.

I said, "Shoot"

I'm not the fastest note-taker in the world, but I knew if I wrote down every fourth or fifth word, I'd be able to read my notes well enough later.

He said he had received a call about an hour ago from Thom Cohen of Ocala, Florida—a man I had met several times in the past. A good friend and funder of the Major's many crusades, Cohen told the Major that his eighteen-year-old daughter, Angela, had not come home from her day trip to Daytona Beach the day before. The friends she was with at the beach said she had left about 1900 that evening, but by 2200, she still had not made it home.

Thom told the Major that he and his wife, Blanche, had tracked her route down Highway US 40 toward the beach and found her car on the side of the road at the intersection of US 40 and State Road 11, near Barberville, Florida. They found the keys in the ignition of the car and her pocketbook on the seat. Thom notified the local Volusia County Sheriff's Office and they were currently investigating. Thom and his wife felt they needed far more help than the Sheriff's office could provide. So, they'd called the Major.

The Major instructed me to drop everything I was doing and fly over to Ocala, interview the Cohens more thoroughly, and find this girl.

I hung up the phone and walked swiftly to the rear of the house. Dave was standing by the bow of his boat. I pushed the remote control next to the back door that locked and alarmed the entire property. As I climbed down into Dave's boat, he passed me my

Smith & Wesson 9MM pistol in a plastic Ziploc bag. He asked me if I needed to file a flight plan or if I was flying visual (VFR). I told him I was headed to Ocala and that I would fly visual.

I stepped to the back of the boat next to Dave as we sped up through Newfound Harbor toward the Merritt Island Airport. I filled him in on what I knew of the case so far. He offered to contact some of his sources from the North Volusia County area to see if there were any rumors skimming around the area. I thanked him and requested that he do just that.

We pulled into Dave's dock behind his house. He grabbed my bag and both of us took off running for my plane parked at the end of the runway. Even though Dave's friend had already completed a preflight on my plane, I repeated the effort, as I always did. I climbed into the left seat and asked Dave to stand by his phone for any instructions. I also asked him to contact my friend Gage Copeland, my intelligence source over at Patrick Air Force Base, and tell him to expect my call as soon as I had more information.

I took off west from the island airport and followed the Indian River until I passed Titusville off my left wing. There, I turned toward the St. Johns River basin. This way I avoided all the commercial air traffic going in and out of the Sanford Orlando International Airport. Forty minutes later, I announced on my radio, to any other plane in the area that I was landing at a private airfield just north of Ocala. I'd gotten permission to use the airfield many years ago by a former client who'd owned it at one time.

I placed a call to Thom while I was on route, advising him to meet me as soon as my wheels touched the tarmac. As I rolled out across the short taxiway, I could see him driving toward me in his black Chevy Suburban. Blanche was sitting in the passenger seat, and I could see, even at this distance, that she looked terrible.

Thom jumped out of his SUV and ran over to my hatch before I even wound down my engine. After I shut down my engine and electronics, I unlocked and pushed my hatch open and greeted Thom under my wing.

After tying my aircraft down, I grabbed Thom by the arm and walked him to his SUV. Blanche, who was standing outside her open passenger door, gave me a quick hug.

She cupped my face between her two hands as she looked up at me. "Please bring my baby home."

The sound of her voice and the look in her eyes choked me up, and I felt like I had never been as motivated to perform a miracle as I was at that moment.

As we rode in Thom's car to his house, he briefed me on everything he knew. When we arrived, he showed me a picture of Angela that, frankly, surprised me. She was of light complexion and very, very blonde, unlike her mother and father, who had dark complexions and dark hair. Blanche noticed my curiosity and told me Angela had been conceived through artificial insemination.

As I stared at this extremely beautiful, blonde young girl in the picture, I began to get a very bad feeling.

After hearing the Cohens' story, I telephoned a couple of Angela's friends who were with her yesterday at the beach. But, other than confirming the time she'd left alone, they were of little help. Paula Davis, the fourth member of the quartet, did not answer her phone, nor did her parents return my call on their answering device. The girl lived close to Silver Springs, so I asked Thom if he would give me a ride to her house.

After assuring Blanche that we would keep her posted, Thom and I drove to Silver Springs.

As we reached the road where the Davis' lived, Thom pointed to the driveway and said, "Those are their two cars."

I asked him to pass the house and stop at the next block. As we went by, I could see Paula through the window, standing in the front room.

Thom pulled over to the side of the road and stopped. I asked him to call Paula's phone again and then her parents'. When no one answered, I nodded to Thom that something was up. He wanted to go up and knock on the door. I advised him to wait. Paula was nineteen years old and no longer a minor. We didn't need her parents' permission to speak with her.

About that time, I received a call from Dave back on Merritt Island. He told me he had spoken with a few of his friends from the North Volusia County area, but no one knew anything about the missing girl. Dave said if it were a kidnapping, these characters would have some knowledge of it. (Dave knows some interesting folks.)

I told Dave about the problem and he suggested it might only be because her parents didn't want her involved for her own safety. I told him he was probably right, but I needed Gage to check the family out as soon as possible.

Gage Copeland is my link to the universe. I have known and worked with him for about forty years. A computer genius with contacts all over the world. Gage is a government employee with more power than anyone I have ever come across. His headquarters and master computers were in the Technology Laboratory on Patrick Air Force Base near Cocoa Beach, Florida. The Tech Lab is across the runway from the Banana River. I can look out any east-facing window of my island home and see the Lab to the east, and he can look west and see my house clearly, but we never planned any of that.

Gage claims my intervention in a problem he was experiencing many years ago saved his life. Frankly, I was just doing what was right for a fellow human being. What does matter is that he's my best friend in the universe and the most important asset I have. Truth be told, he has saved my bacon more times than I can list.

After I talked to Gage, I asked Thom to drive me to an Enterprise Rent-A-Car office, where I rented a small four-wheel drive SUV. He offered to lend me one of his cars, but I was worried about winding up in harm's way.

The next thing I needed to do was view the ground where Angela's car had been found. Not only was it possible for me to pick up on some visual clues, but I might also pick up on some spiritual ones, as well. (Don't ask.)

I drove an hour east to where they had found Angela's car, parked about fifty yards up the road, and walked the rest of the way. Thom pointed out the spot where Angela's car had been found parked partially in the bushes on the south side of the road. She would have been traveling west, so her car should have been on the north side if she pulled over. The location was about one hundred yards west of the crossroad of State Road 11, which had a traffic light at the intersection. I walked back and stood on the westbound side at the light. There was a faded rubber line from the stop line to where Angela's car was found. In fact, it was exactly in line with her car tires and curved, as if her car had been pushed from behind and forced to the left. I asked Thom if there was any damage to her car, and he said he didn't see any, but that she already had some dents on her car. Again, I was getting that same bad feeling.

I asked Thom to call the sheriff's detective who was handling the case and request that he give Thom access to her car. I told him not to mention that he had hired a PI to work the case. Police tend to frown on outside interference. They might start screaming obstruction of an official investigation and try to eat my license.

The detective told Thom where it was and said he would call ahead to give him permission. The car had been towed to a private lot near Barberville on US Route 17. I kicked around a bit more at the scene and then we left. I knew I wanted to come back later to get a little closer to the ground, but without Thom looking over my shoulder. I also wanted to see who was cutting through the woods so frequently that they'd left a fresh trail near where her car was found. I didn't want to drag Thom into any hassle I might encounter, so we took off to the wrecker yard to check out her car.

When we approached the car lot, I saw a man standing near a rear gate. He put his hand up to stop us as we approached. Thom got out and told him he owned the car and had permission from the Sheriff's office to look it over. The man, we later learned, was named Buddy—or maybe that's just what I'd called him when I approached him. I don't recall now, but he answered to it well enough. Ole' Buddy was used to getting his palm scratched from all the DUI folks eager to retrieve the empty booze bottles and hidden drug stashes from under the seat before the Sheriff's Office had an opportunity to inspect.

I walked up to Buddy —perhaps that was when I named him— and said, "Hey, Buddy, is this your twenty I've just found lying on the ground?"

He grabbed it and pushed open the gate for us. He mentioned that the cop who called said there would be a uniformed deputy along shortly to make sure no one tampered with anything before the crime guys finished up with the car. I told him he could count on us to steer clear of any tampering. Buddy took a hike.

As we turned the corner beyond the gate, Thom pointed to a fairly beat up Honda Civic and announced, "Here it is."

Thom had given hundreds of thousands of dollars to Civil Rights groups and more to just Doug's legal campaigns, and his only child was driving a wreck? Thom looked at me, then at the car, and then back to me. "This car is only two years old."

Could have fooled me.

I looked through the car and saw nothing notable until I looked at the rear bumper and the scuffed dirt marks on the trunk lid. The scuffed area was clean of dirt and road dust. The bumper was scraped from recent pressure from behind.

I walked over to the fence and yelled at Buddy if he was the tow operator on the car and he said, "Yes."

I asked him if he towed it frontward or backward. He said from the front. I went back to the car and looked closer. I could see small deposits of rubber or rubber flakes on the scuff marks. I told Thom I had seen enough and said we needed to get gone before the deputy arrived and warned me off of the investigation.

We drove back down to Route 40 and headed west. About a half hour later, Gage called my cell and said he had something interesting for me regarding Mr. and Mrs. Davis. I told him I would call him back in a few minutes and hung up. I didn't want Thom to overhear what Gage had to report, so I looked for a good place to pull over.

We came upon a small store and gas station a couple of miles down the road and I pulled in. I told Thom I needed to call a friend of mine and he should call Blanche and fill her in. I asked him to refrain from mentioning that the Davis' were avoiding us until I had an opportunity to be there with her. I didn't want Blanche rushing over there and accusing them of anything when we had nothing to back it up.

I got out of the car and stood around the back to call Gage back. He answered on the first ring and I could tell he was excited and proud of himself. "Just spit it out," I told him.

Gage said the Davis' had filed bankruptcy some months ago.

Poppa Davis was out of work and Mommy Davis was clerking at a convenience store down in Lake County for minimum wage. They were in debt up to their chins and their house had been on the foreclosure list for a year and was waiting on a court date. I was getting impatient, but I knew I had to endure Gage throwing in one of his famous aphorisms.

"Well, you know money can't buy happiness…but somehow it's more comfortable to cry in a Cadillac than a Yugo." (Ya gotta love 'em.)

He then said that in the last two weeks, the Davis' had paid off many of their debts. They had dropped the bankruptcy case and made up the arrearage on their mortgage payments enough to satisfy the bank. Poppa was still unemployed, but Mommy hadn't shown up for work in a week and a half. But, here comes the best part: Poppa Davis made a flight from Orlando to Brazil and then was back two days later with new luggage and a nice smile for the Customs and Immigration camera. A smile he was looking at right now in the picture lying on his desk.

"But…that's not all. Poppa had a brand new…wait for it…Cadillac."

I thanked Gage and hung up. Time to see the Davis' again, but this time alone and individually.

I drove Thom back to his car near Silver Springs and told him I would call him later. I then called Dave and told him where I was and that I needed two of the largest, ugliest men he knew in Marion County and that I would pay them a hundred dollars each to just stand still and look as menacing as they could. He put me on hold and was back in twenty seconds saying he had two gorillas on their way right now and not to pay them a cent. They owed him money.

Ten minutes after I briefed Dave and hung up, an old Ford pick-up truck pulled up behind me and revved its engine. The windows were tinted so I couldn't tell who was in it, but I decided to take the chance and walked over to it. The doors popped open on both sides and two very large human beings stepped out and grinned at my obvious apprehension.

The truck suspension groaned as they exited, and it gave one last shudder as they slammed the doors.

They both spat tobacco juice out on the ground at the same time and the driver said, "We're Dave's friends."

READ AN EXCERPT OF *SAN ANDROS FAULT* (JAKE STORM #2)

CHAPTER ONE

Lord, this gets tougher all the time.

I have learned not to look directly at the Wall. If I have to, I blur my eyes so I won't focus on any one name. It helps that the Wall is shiny and picks up reflections, blurring the names, but those ghosts draw me in anyway. How could one man recognize so many names that belong to so many faces, so many reaching hands, and so many pleas for help?

Nearly everyone I got close to, everyone that meant something to me…gone. Their spirits reach from beyond and through this wall as if it's their window to get out—to come back to this world. I wish I had the compass, the way, the power to lead them! It sucks the very soul out of me every time I look at the names.

Now, my ghosts use the survivors from the Nam who patrol the Wall to force my attention on them. Their embraces, their words of love, and the camaraderie they display and pass onto me.

What a war! What a nightmare! And, what a daymare it is for me. For me to feel guilty for surviving those three years and the more than a thousand chances to have had my name engraved here. Well, my ghost friends, I gave it my best shot. The bullets could have just as easily hit me. I was right next to you, Johnny. I was standing up, directing fire, when you were hit, Smitty. I know I should have been the target. I don't know why it was you.

Why don't you guys look peaceful? What is it that will finally make you rest? What is it that I can do to make it right? Who can I blame? Why do you call me here and then just reach out? Talk to me! Tell me who to go after. I will just keep moving along this line and hope your messages will eventually break through this thick skull of mine.

I wish I could change my choice of meeting spot with the Major. The Wall is bothering me far more these days than it did years ago. I guess my age is finally wearing on me. All those people I pass along the way, and, on occasion, embrace, look so troubled. My whole life, I have found myself in the wrong place at the right time. Maturity has not changed that.

My name is Jacob Storm. My friends call me Jake. My family calls me Scarce. My enemies don't call me at all. They just drop in from time to time.

As the Vietnam Memorial fades from my right peripheral, I take in the steps of the Lincoln Memorial looming in front of me. One more time, I run the memory tape in my head of the strange story I'd been told the night before on the Ellis Island Ferry by the son of the man currently the subject of my investigation.

His name is Paul Keis. There is no doubt in my mind that the story he related to me is true. It is too bizarre not to be. I even remember the quiet buzz about the incident last month when I was visiting with my friend Calvin Green in Nassau. Calvin is a Bahamas government agent and one of my close friends whom I have known for many years. We have shared more than a few adventures together. It just goes to prove that if a news article or a story catches my attention, somehow, I will become involved in it before too long. Calvin will be invaluable to me in this matter.

When Doug Parton, first signaled me that we needed to talk, I was reluctant, as usual. Our last mission was hairy, and it has taken me nearly six months to heal, both physically and mentally. Doug is an attorney who deals with "less than conventional cases." He has been referred to as the "Don Quixote" of the legal field, and he, in turn, refers to me as his "Help Button."

Over the years, we have been through a great deal together. He mostly handles cases involving civil rights violations, some murder defenses, and many battles against officials of large government agencies that use their position and power to grab money from the average citizen—usually causing great hardship. In some cases, the cause and effect are death and destruction.

I call Doug "The Major" as a code name. I took the name from an old Robert Redford movie we once saw together. It reminded me of what he and I do for a living. The movie was about a group of civilians working for a government agency who were trying to right the wrongs in the world. Only, in our case, we can only "hope" we work for the good guys.

Doug was a Captain in the Army Reserve in college but resigned his commission when they tried to teach him to use a garrote during his Ranger training. He couldn't quite get the hang of it. He thought it was too barbaric.

I felt anxious to get going on this case. The funding was available but would be tight, as usual. But, if I used the Slim Molly, I could cut my expenses to a minimum. The Slim Molly is my thirty-eight-foot Catalina sloop sailboat with a swing keel, modified with a larger-than-usual engine. The swing keel allows me to float over very shallow water. The Big Hat, my fifty-eight-foot Hatteras, was far too expensive, and it would draw too much attention in the area I was heading to. I needed to draw up a plan in my mind and follow it through.

Who was I kidding? I knew as sure as dirt that any plan I devised now I would alter at least ten times over before I even got there. Ol'

Murphy's Law would bite me on the ass as everything changed for the worst—every time it possibly could.

Just then, I spotted the Major, a big man in his own right. I had met him many years before when we both worked for the same law firm in Boston. That wasn't long after he had graduated from law school and before he became the foremost civil rights attorney in the world. He makes a difference in this world, and it's my job to keep him from getting dead and upsetting the balance of the universe.

As he cleared the ridgeline above the wall, I recognized his long gate and surefootedness. I was standing in a shadow with the bright lights of the Lincoln Memorial to my rear as he approached.

After his affectionate hug, he started briefing me on the case. I had already met with the son the night before and had the basic story from him, but the Major filled in the blanks, reemphasizing the importance of a quick and successful conclusion to this matter. He always said that, but I realized he was dead serious this time as the clock was running out on a poor lonely man sitting in a Bahamian prison.

It seemed there were secret goings-on on Andros Island, and the Bahamas government did not want anyone to know about them. It involved the U.S. in a way that would shock the world. The Major was reluctant to speak of it but, finally, after being reminded that I was his best source and comrade in the universe, he filled me in on a long-held U.S.-government secret that there were former Nazi officers living on Andros and that they had been there for many years. I already knew some of the San Andros story but felt it good manners to act as if he was filling me in on incredible new stuff! However, the next bit of information was a shock, even to me. The Major informed me that there were Middle Easterners living there as well and that they had been there since just after the 9/11 World Trade Center disaster!

As quickly as the Major arrived, he disappeared by doing a military about-face and quickly marching into the shadows of the surrounding trees. Before he left, he shouted above the din of the traffic skirting the Capitol Mall, "Don't get dead!"

A common parting wish from him.

CHAPTER TWO

En route to my island home, I went over the electronic files that the Major had sent me earlier. He had requested I catch the next flight up to New York City and meet with the family of an imprisoned man in the Bahamas. The moment I read the Major's email briefing, written in our common code, I was hooked.

The following narrative is the story of Joel Keis, as I know it today from the numerous interviews and documents retrieved from our research. This, to the best of my knowledge, is what Keis had lived through during his tortured and long life.

* * *

Joel Keis, now known as Joel Kelsey—not his legal name but his American adopted one— was a Polish immigrant who came over from Europe after the Second World War. His family and everyone he knew had lived in Kazimierz Doliny, a little Polish town on the eastern banks of the Vistula River in the Lublin Province. Most were Jewish. Under an order from Nazi administrator Adolf Eichmann, all were rounded up in January of 1942 and brought to camps at Treblinka, Belzec, or Sobibor.

These camps were specifically constructed for the extermination of Poland's Jews. All were held in conditions worse than animals. Most were barely clothed, even during the fierce and violent winters. Joel and his family were imprisoned at the Belzec camp. The Germans placed the men in one barbed-wired section and the women and children across the way behind another fenced-in area. Joel could see his wife and three children every day, but he was absolutely forbidden to talk to them or to do anything but make quick eye contact each morning as he headed for the small repair shop where he was forced to work.

Joel and his family were among the millions of Jews and other ethnic people who had been interned in one of the over 42,000 concentration and extermination camps throughout Eastern Europe during the late 1930s through to the middle of the '40s.

Joel would wake up every morning on his hard, wooden bed and, oh so slowly, open his eyes only to realize that his nightmare was a reality. He would glance around at the other half-starved men, careful not to make too much eye contact with them. Most of them resented the fact that he had a job serving the Nazis. What they failed to realize was that Joel's job might be his only chance to save his family. Joel hoped and prayed that he might be able to reach into the hearts of at least some of his captors by cooperating with them.

Joel's job in the small shop was separating gold, platinum, and silver. Some of the precious metals came from the teeth of fallen Jews in his and other nearby camps. He also tested and melted down gold jewelry and separated gems from glass. Joel had been a successful jeweler and gemologist before the Nazis began their campaign of terror in his town.

Nearly every day, Joel would learn that another friend or relative had vanished from the sheds they lived and survived in. Joel worked extremely hard at his task to try to keep in good graces with the camp commandant, a cruel man named Colonel Stefan Braun. It was rumored among the prisoners that Braun's mother was a Jew from Berlin. However, after many months of constant long hours of work, his worst fears were realized. His wife was moved to another shed and, soon thereafter, his children, as well.

He tried frantically to persuade the commandant to bring them back, but he was sent back to his work area with threats of punishment and death if he asked any more questions about his family.

Commandant Braun was a big man. He stood about six-four and was very broad at the shoulders. His tailored uniforms with pads, special cuts, and pleats made him appear even bigger than he actually was, and the highly polished, sterling silver insignias and buttons made him look superior. With almost white-blonde hair, he was often referred to as "The Ghost" by even his own troops. He was younger than Joel by some years and was far younger than many other officers of his rank.

His fierce looks and evil demeanor seemed doubled by the menacing tattoo on the inside of his right forearm depicting a striking snake wrapped around a double-edged dagger—a decoration he proudly wore exposed, keeping the sleeves of his tunic folded up at all times, including on the most severely cold days of the Polish winters. Braun took perverse pleasure in tormenting his prisoners. Every prisoner was made to stare at this ugly display of painted terror as he toured the shacks and work areas of the camps, making sure his supremacy was understood—but mostly feared.

One day, as Joel was scanning the faces of the people being forced into the open-backed trucks near the perimeter of the camp, he spied his wife looking back at him. She was, as were many of the others, completely nude and being struck by one of the guards as she tried to call to him. Joel broke from the work line and ran to her across the field as she was thrown into the bed of the truck.

As he approached the truck and saw how tortured her face looked, he knew she was probably being transported to one of the many death pits he had heard about from the other prisoners. As he ran to her, a guard struck him on the back of his head with his rifle butt and knocked him to the ground. All hope left Joel that day. He never saw any member of his family again. And, every night, Joel dreamed of Braun's snake tattoo. He knew it was probably the last thing his wife and children had seen before they were placed alive in the death trenches of the camp and then burned.

Joel thought he would never forget that day in 5702, a date based on the Hebrew calendar, as it marked what he thought was the end of happiness for him. The years drifted by like a nightmare as Joel barely survived starving to death. His skills were the only reason they allowed him to live, but he prayed for a quick death every night.

One day Joel woke up to the sound of shouting by the guards and people screaming for mercy. Joel quickly ran to his little shop only to see it had been ransacked of all the gold and precious stones he had divided the day before. He looked through the window to see the guards forcing hordes of prisoners into the death trucks and driving toward the death trenches at high speeds, a sight he had never seen before. There were far too many prisoners running from the wooden sheds to fit in the trucks, even though there were many trucks staged for loading.

All of a sudden, the guards fired their rifles into the crowds of prisoners just as fast as they could. The guards kept reloading their rifles and firing at point-blank range at anything that moved. Joel ran from his shop and picked up a long-handled shovel and began swinging and pounding and slicing the guards from behind until the prisoners, the ones still able to walk, rushed the guards, whom they outnumbered twenty to one. The prisoners tore the guard's limb from limb with their bare hands. The entire camp became a bloody battlefield as the prisoners picked up the guards' weapons and began shooting every uniform they could see.

After what seemed like hours of horrific battle, Joel and the rest of the prisoners—some two or three thousand of them—found themselves standing in the blood-soaked field at the center of the camp with no guard left standing. The only sounds were the crying and whimpering of those dying and the sounds of some of the prisoners who had turned the weapons on themselves.

In the distance, Joel could hear artillery booming and the sounds of explosions as the rounds struck their mark. The prisoners figured it was the Germans coming to finish them off.

Joel re-loaded the rifle he was carrying and ran over to the headquarters building to look for the commandant and his staff. When he entered the building, he saw the commandant's office was empty of all memorabilia and files. There wasn't a trace of the monster left anywhere. Joel looked at the rifle he was holding and thought of his family and friends lying in the cold, dark earth beyond the barbed-wire fence that still loomed from horizon to horizon. One small pull of the trigger with the barrel to his head and he would join his family, but he quickly put that thought out of his head and focused on the missed opportunity to put the monster down. Joel felt robbed once again as he looked out the window at his last chance for revenge.

Within a couple of hours, some small fighter planes flew over—

not German but American Bell P-63 King Cobras and British Hawker Typhoon fighters. The pilots were taking photographs of the people on the ground from the canopies. It seemed as though there were hundreds of planes flying toward the east in the direction of the Germans' retreating lines of military trucks and small Volkswagen cars.

Later that day, an American Army group came to the camp. It took a while for the Americans to convince the armed prisoners that they were there to help. Eventually, they let them into the camp to treat the sick and wounded.

Although many of Joel's campmates died in the coming days from wounds received during the take-over battle or just disease in general, the American forces fed, clothed, and nursed many of them back to health. Joel needed very little care, as he was one of the few who'd been given a steady diet due to his value as a tradesman.

Joel found himself the center of attention, as he was one of the longest-lived survivors in the camp. It was also soon discovered that he had a vast knowledge of the Germans' business dealings, as well as their leadership. Joel was quickly transferred to the area command center and eventually to the Allied Operational and Occupation Headquarters in London, England.

Before he had left the camp, he searched endlessly through piles of dead Germans for The Ghost and his staff but was unable to find even one member of the camp command.

Joel stayed in England for a number of months after the war as an advisor to the Allied Forces. He was then given the opportunity to return to Poland or relocate to the United States of America, where he had a distant cousin in Brooklyn. Joel had been briefed by some late arrivals from Poland that the Russians were now taking over Poland and were not much kinder to the Jews and the Poles than the

Germans had been. It did not take Joel long to choose the United States as his new home.

Joel moved in with his cousin and his family in New York. As the economy once again began to grow and prosper, he soon found employment in the vast diamond and jewelry district of Manhattan on West 47th Street.

Joel met a young Jewish girl named Adrian, whose husband had been killed in the war in Europe some years before. Their relationship flourished, seemed to take on a life of its own, and soon they were married with three children—Paul, Josh, and last, but certainly not least, sweet little Katy.

Joel worked very hard at his trade and his hard work paid off. In the late fifties, he started his own business. Fifty years later, his children finally convinced him to work fewer hours and spend more time at home with their mother.

Joel and Adrian had many friends in Brooklyn. Many had lived through the death camps of Europe and migrated to the U.S. for a new start in life, but hardly spoke of the horrible camps. As the children of the Holocaust survivors grew up and began asking questions about the numbers tattooed on the adult's arms, the survivors began to share some of the stories. Many of the children hid in corners and covered their eyes and ears on hearing the horror stories. Joel and the others' stories of "The Ghost" and his sadistic tattoo especially enthralled them.

Joel, Adrian, Paul, Josh, and Katy all had good lives. His sons both became attorneys and his daughter Katy was the wild one. She was more of a tomboy than her two brothers. She became a firefighter for the City of New York. They were a happy family.

Then came 9/11. At about 9:00 AM that morning, Adrian called Joel to tell him to turn on the local TV channel. That evening, two firefighters from Katy's unit knocked on the door to tell them Katy had been inside the North Tower when it collapsed. Joel could hardly breathe.

As Joel fell to his knees, the question: "Why me again?" ran through every vein of his being.

The following days, nights, and weeks after losing Katy were agonizing. It was all a grim reminder of his days in the prison camps when he knew his entire family was gone and that he would never see or hold them again.

Joel's faith and his wife, Adrian, kept him going, but the hatred he felt inside toward the monsters, whether they were Arabs or members of a great conspiracy who had perpetrated these events, was overwhelming.

Ted Lowell and his wife, Debbie, were close friends of Joel and Adrian. Ted was a concentration camp survivor like Joel. Joel trusted Ted completely and they often consulted one another in matters of personal feelings and family.

Since Ted was retired, he and Debbie had decided to do some traveling. They went to their local Thomas Cook Travel Agent regarding a trip they were planning to the Caribbean. The travel agent told them that she and her husband had stayed on Andros Island within the past year and enjoyed its remoteness and lush, sandy beaches. She explained that Andros is the largest island in the Bahamas—104 miles long and forty miles wide, with the third-largest barrier reef in the world. She highly recommended it. Ted and Debbie took an off-season trip to the coastal village of Nichols Town near the northeast coast of Andros Island in the southern Bahamas.

Ted and Debbie traveled to Nassau on Bahamas Air and then on to Andros by commuter plane landing in the small San Andros Airport a few, short miles west of Nichols Town. Ted was able to rent an old Volkswagen Beetle from a local resident who happened to be a German. He happily took the car rather than rent a moped, as he would surely injure himself.

On the day before they left to come home, Ted put a small, but quite visible, dent in the right rear fender of their rental Volkswagen. Ted inquired of the motel manager where he could find the German fellow who had rented him the car so he could pay for the damages before he traveled back to the US. After receiving the directions, he left Debbie at the motel and drove toward the town of San Andros.

He was surprised to find that the village of San Andros was a fairly modern housing area equal to many housing developments in the rural USA. He noticed that many homes had garages, carports, and front porches. Ted even saw a modern general store. The only difference was that most of the directional signage, street signs, and window ads were written in German and Arabic.

Ted stopped at the store and inquired of the men relaxing on the porch where he could find the VW's owner. He was instructed in very broken English to drive to the Community Center down the road and inquire there. Much help they were not!

Ted drove a bit farther and came to a sentry shack with a closed gate. The sentry only glanced at the old VW and motioned him through as he opened the gate. Ted turned the next corner and saw what appeared to be a Mosque. There were men and women in Arabic garb walking toward the Mosque. Many of the homes were modern and looked like elaborate U. S. homes. Some of the men waved at the car as Ted drove by but didn't seem to pay much attention to who was driving. Ted figured that was why the guard at the gate did not stop him.

He drove to the end of the road but still did not see any building that resembled a Community Center. Ted turned around and drove back toward the sentry gate. As he passed the Mosque, he saw a man who looked remarkably like Osama Bin Laden standing with two other men. At least the man looked like the pictures Ted had seen of Bin Laden, just not as tall.

Ted had his camera on the seat next to him as he had been taking shots of the local landscape. He picked up his camera and shot a number of quick photos, keeping the camera low. As he started to drive off, one of the men with the Bin Laden look-alike who appeared to be the size of a Detroit Lions linebacker looked directly at Ted and started to run toward the vehicle. Ted drove off quickly, heading directly to the gate.

Ted stopped in front of the gate and asked the sentry, who appeared to be an American soldier, where the Community Center was. The sentry became wide-eyed and asked him to exit the area immediately!

Ted drove to a large building with a group of men standing outside talking. Once again, he inquired about the whereabouts of the car owner. He was directed to a small house just down the way. As he left the men in front of the building, he saw a large man walking toward them from the other direction. The man, elderly but still huge and muscular, glared menacingly at Ted as he approached. As Ted drove off, he noticed something that turned his blood to ice water. The man had a tattoo of a snake wrapped around a dual-edged dagger on the inside of his right forearm.

Ted stared too long. The man began walking toward him. Ted placed the car in gear, hit the gas pedal, and drove toward the small house the men had directed him to. When he stopped a short distance away he took out his camera, snuck back between the houses, and snapped five or six pictures of the group in front of the store, including the large, elderly man with the tattoo.

Ted returned to the car with the camera and quickly changed the film, placing the exposed roll neatly under the seat where it was hidden but easily accessible. As he climbed out of the car, two large young men grabbed him and forcibly relieved him of his camera.

The men spoke to him in German, popped open the back of the camera, and pulled the film from it. They then threw the camera into the car, breaking it into three pieces. They strong-armed Ted and pushed him back into the car. Despite the men's German, which he spoke very little of, he understood they wanted him to leave the area immediately. In the rearview mirror, Ted could see the large man with the tattoo speaking with one of the Arabic men he had seen earlier. The Arab was pointing toward Ted and the car.

Ted drove quickly out of the settlement and back to the motel.

Ted and Debbie flew home the next day. Ted continually spoke of his encounter with the muscular old German with the tattoo and the Middle Eastern men near the Mosque. Ted had thankfully retrieved the film from under the seat of the old VW and had it safely stored in his carry-on bag. This film was not leaving his side!

After arriving back in New York, Ted had all their vacation film rolls processed. A couple of weeks later, Ted and Debbie contacted their friends and invited them to view their wonderful vacation photos of San Andros and to celebrate Joel and Adrian's wedding anniversary. The Saturday night get-together was well underway when Ted took out the envelopes containing the vacation photos. All were amazed to see the land crabs that crawled all over Andros Island like large insects. They were just as amazed at the beauty of the island edged in sugar sand and surrounded by turquoise-colored water with coral reefs visible just below the surface.

As Ted randomly flipped through the photos, he came upon the ones he'd shot in the village community of San Andros. When he flipped to the picture of the large German man, Joel gasped, grabbed the photo from Ted with both hands, and fell to the floor next to the coffee table, his whole body shaking. He would not respond to Adrian's pleas to tell her what was wrong. Everyone was convinced he was having a stroke.

Ted suddenly realized the photo was of the monster that Joel had described in the camp during the war—"The Ghost" who was such a brutal part of Joel's nightmares. Ted got Joel off the floor by telling him, "Now justice can be served and God will lead the way."

All that night and through the next day, Joel locked himself away in his office and pored over every reference book he could find regarding the Bahamas. He called the Bahamas' Consulate Office in New York City to inquire about the village of San Andros on Andros Island. He called Ted many times throughout the day to question him further about the tattooed old man and to see if there was anything else Ted could recall of his encounter

Ted had consulted a lawyer friend, named Chris, about the Arabs and had found that the Bin Laden look-alike could possibly be Osama's older brother, Salem Bin Laden who had been living in Orlando at the time of the attack on the World Trade Center. Mysteriously, he and a group of Middle Easterners had been allowed to fly out of the Orlando International Airport after the attacks, when all the other flights were grounded and all U.S. airspace had been closed. Chris had a source within the government that helped him often with information for his clients.

The plane must have flown all those Middle Easterners directly to the Bahamas under our government's sanction since all flights had been grounded at that time. Chris said he would contact one of his friends to see if he could find out anything. He told Ted to be patient as information of this nature took time to uncover.

Joel's research on San Andros wasn't very useful. The town magically appeared without any fanfare around the end of the 1940s. There were no resident listings, just a post office reference in nearby Nicholls Town. There was, however, a mention of a Canadian consulate contact in San Andros at Morgan's Bluff, in the Nicholls Town tourist reference.

The next morning, Joel went to the Canadian Consulate's Office in Manhattan and inquired about their knowledge of the village of San Andros. No one at the consulate knew anything about San Andros or had any contacts there.

Joel knew that he was going to have to go to Andros to see for himself. Adrian came home from work to find Joel packing. She asked him if she could go with him, but Joel explained that this was something he just had to do alone. He did not know what was going to happen and did not want to place Adrian in harm's way.

The next morning, Joel left JFK for Miami and then secured a private charter to San Andros airport. The flight was shorter then Joel had anticipated. Suddenly, he was on the tarmac at the San Andros airport. A feeling rushed over him like something he had not felt since the day the American troops entered the concentration camp and he realized the Nazis in charge of the camp had slipped by the troops and wiggled their way to safe passage.

Once Joel got his motel room there at the airport, he arranged for a moped and secured a full-face helmet. The full helmet was going to work well to hide his face and protect his identity, but with the searing San Andros heat, it was going to be like wearing Hell on his head!

Back in Brooklyn, Ted received a call from his lawyer friend Chris. He asked Ted if he would mind sharing his vacation photos with another lawyer he knew in Washington, D.C. Ted agreed and asked to be kept in the loop about any information.

In San Andros, Joel drove toward Nicholstown. As he rode along the bumpy asphalt road, he passed only one other vehicle coming the other way. It was dark and quiet like a cemetery feels at night. He slowly came to a stop on the side of the road. He could make out a slight reflection, not much light but just enough to know something was up ahead. Joel pulled off the road, parked the Moped deep in the trees, and continued on foot.

Soon, he could hear voices speaking German. It made his stomach turn. Joel crept through the brush and recognized the voice of the "The Ghost," something Joel thought was never going to happen until he chased him to hell after he passed away!

A group of about ten or so men stood next to a building, arguing in German, which Joel spoke fluently, about expenses for some kind of travel they were planning to take in the near future. They were talking about flights out of Miami and New York.

Joel cautiously moved as close as he could to the voices and found a car parked near the first building. He was relieved that no interior light or sound gave him away as he slipped inside the rear seat. As he peered up through the window, he saw, standing no more than ten feet away, Commandant Braun and two other men coming from the building. As he stared at the Monster, Braun turned and stared right at the car as if he sensed Joel's presence and his loudly beating heart. Soon, the commandant and his mates walked away into the night.

Joel was sure he had been detected, and he knew he had to leave immediately or he'd be caught.

As Joel slid out of the car and to the ground, he felt a hard, steel rod lying on the floorboard. He carried the tire iron with him to the brush, and just as he arrived at the edge of the woods, he heard the breaking of twigs. He turned just in time to see the commandant swinging a long shiny blade of sorts at him. It happened so fast that it was like a bolt of lightning and it nicked his left shoulder and struck the tree next to him, nearly cutting the sapling clear through. Joel tried to duck and run, but the blade nicked him a second time as he turned.

The aging man's condition caught Joel off guard. He had to be in his late seventies, but was still agile enough to keep swinging the sword repeatedly! But, as Joel stumbled backward, he noticed the Monster's legs seemed to weaken with every step and his eyes appeared to be clouded with cataracts. Still, he could clearly see the fury in the commandant's face.

Joel kept stepping backward faster and faster in the brush but lost his footing and fell backward. The commandant took one more huge step and lifted the shining blade over his head to finish Joel off…when he tripped and fell forward. Instinctively, Joel threw his hands up to block the huge man from falling directly on him, holding the tire iron up to protect himself. As the commandant fell, the tire iron jammed into the commandant's left eye and continued to pierce his head, nearly coming out the back of his skull. The sound of the bone shattering in his skull was like nothing Joel had ever heard before.

Joel was terrified! He had always dreamed of killing this Monster, this beast, who had robbed him of his life and family in Poland. Now, he had killed "The Ghost" and, at present, he was pinned under the large man's lifeless body.

It was getting harder to breathe. He strained to push the dead body off him and nearly slid out from under the weight when flashlights seemed to be coming from all directions, shining on him and the prone body on the ground. One of the older men with a flashlight began to shout to the others standing near the community building. Soon, all came running. Joel mustered up as much strength as he could, crawled to his feet, and ran as fast as possible toward the Moped hidden in the trees. Joel realized he was feeling extremely weak and his thoughts were getting foggy as he moved through the ambient lights of the nearby buildings. He could see his clothes were turning red from his blood loss!

Joel was only able to take five more steps when he ran out of energy and collapsed face-first to the ground. He could see the back reflector of the moped in the bushes just a few steps away but someone struck him on his back with something hard. Just before he lost consciousness, he heard someone screaming that Braun was dead.

Joel woke up lying on a steel bed with the smell of antiseptic in the air. He was handcuffed to the bed with an IV running into his arm. He attempted to sit up but was far too weak to move.

A small black man came over and examined his arm and shoulder. It was then that Joel noticed he was in great pain. Joel asked the man where he was and why he was handcuffed to the bed. The man introduced himself as Dr. James Whittington and explained to Joel that he was in a village clinic near Nicholstown on Andros Island.

The altercation with the commandant came crashing back to Joel. The doctor explained that Joel had been unconscious for two days and that as soon as the doctor felt he was strong enough to make the journey, Joel would be transferred into the custody of a constable coming in from Nassau

Although the doctor did not know the exact nature of the charges against Joel, he explained that they were serious enough that only the doctor and his nursing assistant were allowed to treat him or speak to him directly. That included the local Constables from Andros Island.

The doctor told Joel that the night before, an expensive-looking twin-engine aircraft had flown in from Miami and a number of very important looking men met in one of the hangars next to the airfield. He said the men were Americans, wanted to take custody of Joel. The Doctor told him that he had to threaten them with a call to his family, who were very important people in Nassau, to prevent these men from moving Joel out of the clinic.

The doctor had put 140 stitches in his arms and shoulder and told Joel that he had very serious, life-threatening injuries. He advised Joel to move carefully or the stitches wouldn't hold. Although Joel heard most of what the doctor was saying, with all the medication and pain, he fell back asleep, never imagining what the future held for him.

Back home, Adrian was frantic. She had been calling the motel every hour only to be told that Joel had not made it back to his room in the three days since he had checked in. The desk clerk said that Joel rented a moped, but that was all Adrian could gather.

After speaking with the desk clerk, the hotel manager, Paul Messing, realized that something was wrong. He contacted Adrian and told her that he would call a friend of his in San Andros to inquire further and would update her when he had any information.

Messing reported Joel missing but the local constable told him that they had no knowledge of Joel's whereabouts—or any other information regarding him. Meanwhile, Adrian called an old friend, Mary Koskoff, whom she had known many years ago from Harvard College and asked for advice. Professor Koskoff was the Dean of The Harvard School of Law and had always been a great advocate of Human Rights, especially regarding governmental abuse of power.

After Adrian explained what Joel was doing in the Bahamas and about his mysterious disappearance, Mary immediately agreed to assist Adrian. Mary called a friend of hers at the State Department and learned that there was, in fact, an incident in the Bahamas. He told Mary that although he did not have any additional information, the Secretary of State herself was personally involved and he would try to learn more.

Later that same day, an orderly led Joel out a back door and into the bed of a small truck. Joel saw two black men wearing brand-new suits standing about ten feet away, speaking American English—no accents. He quickly walked to them, but one of the black guards who were with the suits struck him violently from behind. As Joel fell to the ground, he saw the two men look the other way. He was beginning to feel a very old but familiar fear. The location had changed, the men had changed, but these men pulling him to his feet were just as callous, vicious, and dangerous as the ones in Poland.

Two large black men forced Joel into the rear of the truck and told him to lie down and not to look up. They drove off, and when they stopped a few moments later, Joel could see through a crack in the aged, green canvas covering the back of the truck that the two men in the suits were now speaking with one of the old men from the little German settlement, as well as an Arab man wearing a turban. They did not look at all happy as they watched the truck drive away.

Joel could tell that they were driving toward the airport because the turquoise blue ocean was to his right. Soon, they slowed and Joel could see his motel where his few belongings must still be located. That was the least of his worries as they passed into the airport. As they came to an abrupt stop, a propeller plane engine coughed to life. The next few hours would match any horror Joel had ever experienced in his life.

Adrian received a call back from Mary Koskoff about ten o'clock that same night telling her that her source had been informed that an unnamed American was being detained in the Bahamas for the murder of a Canadian citizen living in the Bahamas. The U.S. State Department was not releasing any information at this time and was leaving the matter to the Bahamian officials to handle as they saw fit.

It wasn't until two days later that Joel was informed that he was being officially charged with the premeditated murder of Stephan Braun. He was not allowed to make a phone call or speak with a lawyer. Still in handcuffs, he was flown to a small airstrip and then transported to a large, gray cement building balanced on a coral reef on the shore of a large island. Once the handcuffs were removed and he could see around him, Joel realized he was alone in a small cell. He could see out of a small, barred window toward the open ocean. The view was peaceful, but the rest of the accommodations and level of service was not.

Adrian took the morning train into the city to confront the Bahamas consul in person. She had been put off long enough by telephone. Paul Keis, Joel's eldest son (he had rejected the name change to Kelsey), flew to New York from his home in London to be with his mother and to try to find his father and bring him home. The Bahamians at the consulate were just as confused as Adrian was and claimed they could not help.

Paul Keis was a barrister in England with many influential friends in the legal community. One of these friends was Doug Partin. Paul called Doug from the airport as soon as he landed and explained what he knew so far. Doug had visited Paul's father and mother many times over the years and was concerned by the news. He immediately offered to help.

Joel, meanwhile, was sitting in his cell, going over the events of the past three days. He kept thinking back to the two Americans at the clinic and the way they turned and looked away when the guards assaulted him. He was sure they were U.S. officials and were there because of him. The more he thought about it, the more confused he became.

He asked the prison officials if he could see someone from the American Embassy, but he was told repeatedly that they had been notified and that they did not want to get involved. He was also told that he could see an attorney as soon as one was located to take on his case. Joel asked them many times to call his family. He even explained that his son, Paul, was a lawyer in Great Britain and could represent him here in the Bahamas. They did not allow him any calls—and told him he would lose any future privileges if he persisted in asking. Silence seemed to be the best policy, at least for the immediate future.

Paul met Doug Parton near the front door of the Bahamas Consulate Office in New York City. As they waited for Adrian to arrive from Penn Station, Paul filled Doug in on everything he knew at this point. Paul had called the Bahamas Prosecutor's Office before he left Heathrow for Kennedy, but he was told they had no knowledge of a Joel Keis and did not have him in their custody. They said they would look into it and call him back before his plane left. Paul never received the call. He called them again as soon as his plane touched down on the tarmac. After being rerouted through numerous people at the Prosecutor's Office, he was told that they had no knowledge of his father.

Doug took out his cell phone and called a familiar number from memory. Jake Storm! While Doug spoke, Paul heard his old friend speaking in some form of code as they arranged to meet near "the curbstone." Doug turned to Paul and said that he would know much more by the end of the day. Doug seemed pretty sure of himself…and confident in the man he had called.

HOMEWARD ANGELS

* * *

I called Dave, my right- and left-hand man, at his little house near my island in the Banana River near Cape Canaveral, Florida, and asked him to prep the Molly for a two-week cruise. I also asked him to load my weapons into the secret compartments in the gunnels. Dave knew exactly what I would need for this kind of trip.

Dave and I had planned to fly up to Ashburn, Georgia, in my Cessna 182 for a couple of days relaxing and eating at the best barbecue restaurant in the south, Keith-A-Que's, and I know Dave was disappointed in the change of plans, but he would never show it. Keith's place is a safe meeting place for my sources and me in that section of the south. Not only is Ashburn a safe and relaxing hideaway, but it is also surrounded by military bases and some of the great intelligence minds in the entire world. After I got underway, Dave could fly up and smooth things over with the folks there and also see if they had any knowledge of the goings-on at Andros Island.

For me, my first stop would be Andros to see what I could find out about this German village and why there were Arab folks next door. The second part of the case would involve backing up Doug as he wound his way through the legal process in Nassau. Watching Doug is always interesting. He appears to grow more and more knowledgeably clever every year. Doug gets himself into lots of bad spots and very seldom cares what it costs. He has little regard for his own safety as he wallows in the legal mud. This time it was far more intriguing than the normal everyday venture.

I could sense that someone in a high place was nervous about this matter and was already gathering information about my whereabouts. I had received a text message from a good friend with Homeland Security that my name had become more prominent on the watch list with some obscure government agency.

As soon as I arrived at my parking spot on South Tropical Drive opposite my island, Dave picked me up in his boat and excitedly told me about a black helicopter that had buzzed the island with four passes and then flew toward the Tech lab at Patrick Air Force Base.

I immediately called my friend Gage Copeland from the Intel office at the Tech Lab on Patrick Air Force Base, and he told me that a couple of spooks were down from D.C. and had asked a lot of questions about me. Gage is one of my very best and most trusted friends, as well as my "information guru." If information is out there to see, hear, know—or even if it is not—Gage can and will find it.

I figured the spooks were trying to decide if I was ashore. That did not bode well for our safety. Somehow, we had stepped into a hornet's nest by my preliminary inquiries, and we hadn't even started our formal investigation yet.

It was about 23:00 and a good time to slip anchor and head out. With any luck, I could be gone and fifty miles out to sea before first light. That meant that I would have to shoot Sebastian Inlet in the dark. With an offshore wind, that was going to be rough!

ABOUT THE AUTHOR

William Johnstone Taylor has been an active investigator for more than forty years and is the Director of the William J. Taylor Agency. He was Chief Investigator and a consultant on a number of high-publicity cases, including The Karen Silkwood case, featured in the movie *Silkwood*, the kidnapping and murder of Charles Harmon in Santiago, Chile, depicted in the movie *Missing*, and many other nationally and internationally renowned investigations.

Mr. Taylor is a former Marine Corps Criminal Investigator and Intelligence Officer. He served three tours of duty in the Republic of South Vietnam. He has been a featured speaker for The Association of American Trail Lawyers, Florida Bar Association, Pace University School of Law, Connecticut Bar Association, and many other organizations throughout the years.

Mr. Taylor is a Lifetime Member of The Federal Criminal Investigators Association, a past member of the International Police Congress, a former member of the Florida Secretary of State Private Security Council, Florida Association of Licensed Investigators, Central Florida Criminal Justice Council, Private Investigators Association of Florida, and Past President of the Florida Association of Private Investigators.

Stolen Angels was his first Jake Storm novel. *San Andros Fault* is his second.

He lives in Pickens County, Georgia, with his wife, dog, and two cats.

Made in the USA
Columbia, SC
02 February 2025